I0659277

First Paperback Edition, 2010
Published in Canada
Book design: D.Grîn

Cover art, illustrations and author portrait: © 2010 David Aronson
www.alchemicalwedding.com

ISBN: 978-1-926617-04-6

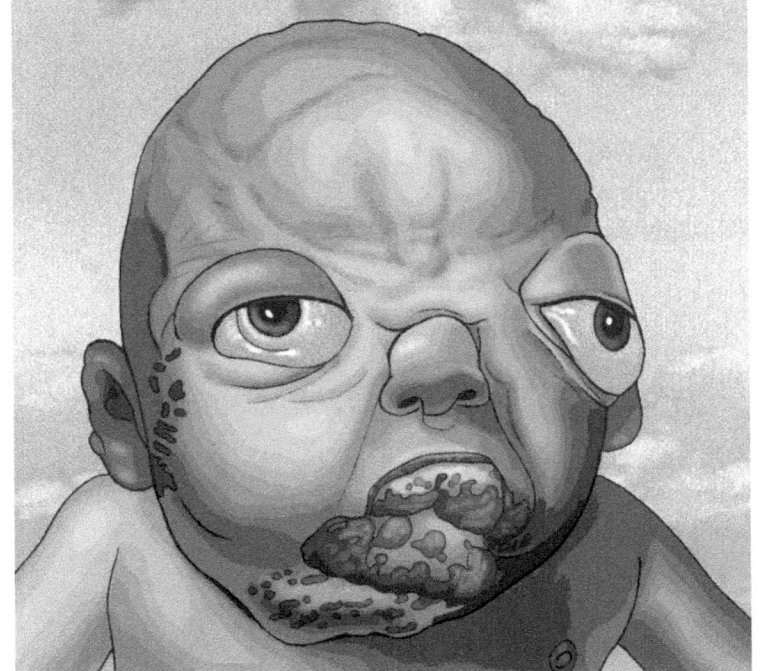

BOMB BABY

TOM BRADLEY

TABLE OF CONTENTS

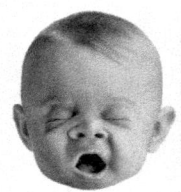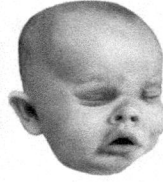

...in the day of atonement shall ye make the trumpet sound. And ye shall hallow the fiftieth year, and proclaim liberty throughout all the land, unto all the inhabitants thereof. It shall be a Jubilee unto you, and ye shall return every man unto his possession, and ye shall return every man unto his family.

— Leviticus 25:9-10

I.

An unwed mother moves along the mud alleys of eighteenth-century Hiroshima, keeping in the shadows. She carries a bundled-up pair of newborn twins.

She creeps along the back wall of an ancient Buddhist temple and approaches the baby abandonment drawer—standard equipment for institutions such as these. Sunken into the wall just above ground level, it's designed to accommodate up to a half-dozen unwanted infants at a time.

The unwed mother deposits her sleeping burdens in the drawer and gives it a gentle shove, sending them through to the other side of the wall.

In the safety of the temple enclosure, a shaven-headed monk meditates at the edge of an ornamental lotus pond. Roused from his prayers by the babbling of the new arrivals, he goes to collect them.

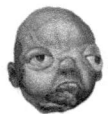

Tom Bradley

A couple hundred years later, the atom bomb arrives and flattens the temple, except for the back wall.

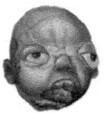

Less than one year later, Catholic missionaries are overseeing the construction of a cathedral on the former site of the temple. They are incorporating the old wall as a memorial of the blast.

Work proceeds very slowly, as everybody suffers from radiation sickness, except for a young, burly Catalonian priest called Father Gaudi.

In the night shadows behind the new cathedral, a Japanese woman, broiled by gamma rays, tucks something in the baby abandonment drawer. Weeping, she limps off into the scorched rubble.

She makes her way to the bank of the shallow river that flows sluggishly as mucus through the ruined city. She crawls onto a makeshift raft, shoves weakly off, and drifts into the smoky darkness, moaning, dying.

Bomb Baby

The next morning Father Gaudi is laboring on his vegetable garden in the radioactive churchyard soil. He can get nothing to grow but nameless weeds with little blue flowers.

He hears odd sounds coming from a tangle of weeds along the back wall. It sounds like a baby, more or less.

II.

It's Sunday morning, August sixth, 1995: exactly half a century after the bomb.

A lavish Japanese wedding party is gathering in the cathedral compound. A professional video crew, formally dressed, tapes the whole affair.

Calling most of the shots is Ishida-san, proud father-of-the-bride and local crime boss. He wears an anachronistic morning coat with tails and pinstriped pants. White-button spats cling to his glossy shoes. Slightly bored, he flips an expensive, half-smoked cigar into the parking lot. It lands behind a black stretch limo and sizzles in a red puddle of transmission fluid.

Beyond the limo, a poinsettia bush grows against the back wall, more or less concealing the baby abandonment drawer. It opens a crack, and a tiny face peeks in from the street. A little blackened hand reaches out and slides the drawer all the way open on its squeaking runners, revealing a simple-minded, malformed bum. The bomb baby has wadded himself into the baby-sized chute, like a contortionist, using every square centimeter of space.

Bomb Baby

Silently and rapidly, he smuggles himself into the churchyard, and heads for the cigar. A few crows swoop down from the gray sky.

After a struggle, the bomb baby emerges from behind the limo. He's brushing black feathers off his rags and chewing on the cigar. Mumbling contentedly, he approaches the wedding party with intentions of mingling.

Parked at the side of the cathedral are five or six flashy vans belonging to the Yakuza. Filipinas and Filipino transvestites hang out of the windows, chatting. They are prostitutes enslaved by Ishida-san's organization. The transvestites are in full drag, their Sunday best.

Yakuza thugs fidget behind the steering wheels of the vans. They wear dark glasses. Colorful dragon tattoos peek from under the cuffs of their rental tuxedos.

A couple dozen expatriated foreigners from every part of the world are descending the side steps that lead to the crypt chapel. Among them is Hank, an American. He is dressed in a stonewashed brushed-denim suit, a chic auburn ponytail sprouting meticulously from the back of his coiffed head. His position in the R&D department of a major automotive company requires this appearance of unconventionality and creativity kept under tight wraps.

With him, or at least next to him, is a tall, strong-looking woman named Polly Edwine, also an American, to whom Hank comments, "It's nice to see the girls get a little air. But why are the thugs dressed up so fancy?"

"In case they're needed to quell disturbances at the wedding. Their boss is marrying off his oldest daughter."

"No, really?" says Hank, squinting at the wedding party. "Is that him?"

"That's the great Ishida-san."

"He does look more angular than most fathers-of-the-bride, now that you mention it."

"It comes from sampling his own shipments of methedrine."

"Does he sample his own shipments of Filipinas? They'll rent this dump to anybody!"

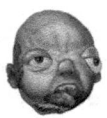

Inside the crypt chapel, a Nigerian acolyte props a fake silk screen in front of the altar. The customary Sunday morning social hour gets underway. It's a regular Tower of Babel. A single language, English, echoes among the pews, but it's an English rich with an astounding array of accents.

Hank rousts a slightly emaciated, extremely pregnant Chinese boat person from a folding chair in the back, and confiscates the few thin cushions upon which the poor girl was sitting. He hustles them up to the front pew, for the benefit of a bevy of white ladies who have staked out the most pious place in the crypt for themselves. These are the

Bomb Baby

American automotive executives' wives. Their husbands, Hank's bosses, are in Hiroshima pursuing gargantuan joint-venture deals.

Hank joins Polly in a pew further back. He says, "The faithful are banished to the basement so Ishida-san can desecrate the place with his daughter."

Polly replies, "You're not one of the faithful. The grand dames drag you here."

"They need a man to protect them from the underworld figures."

"What about their husbands?"

"On the golf course with Japanese counterparts. Automotive joint venture is a most delicate affair."

"I can imagine."

"Luckily for me, I'm in the creative end of things. Nobody expects me to know my chipper from my putter. I'm allowed to spend my only free day worshiping."

Hank picks up a hymnal and pretends to ponder some inspirational verses. He offers to share with Polly.

"In other words, Hank, your masters' wives drag you here. By the ponytail."

"Well, you drag your hubby here, too. At least as far as the parking lot. Isn't that where you left the professor? Sleeping off Saturday night in the family death trap?"

"Who says he's sleeping? Sammy could be praying out there among the thugs."

"Or magically levitating that poor Mazda three feet in the air. With him inside, the shocks could use a rest."

Giggling is heard, and a clatter of spike heels, as three Filipinas come scurrying down the stairs to join the party.

Tom Bradley

They are welcomed by everyone, except the automotive wives, who consider themselves too good to pray with mere prostitutes.

The Nigerian acolyte grins over a dewy armload of white altar flowers and says, "Finally, the mobsters let some lovelies escape from the vans."

"No, we sneaked away in the madness. Something wonderful is happening up there! Everybody come! It's wonderful! You must come see!"

Everyone, except the automotive wives, scampers out.

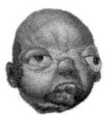

The wedding has been disrupted. Thugs, in formal dress, armed with lead pipes and jack handles, are chasing the bomb baby around, at the instigation of Ishida-san. They are terrified of coming into contact with such an unlucky creature, but they fear the wrath of their boss just as much.

With much agility and speed, the bomb baby scales the compound wall. He perches on top, hooting and jeering. Ishida-san's cigar stub is still clenched between his lips, and it oozes transmission fluid down his chin. He bumps and grinds like a Filipina stripper in a Yakuza nightclub.

The foreigners watch from the safety of the crypt steps. They cheer the bomb baby on as he prances along the top of the wall.

"Sanctuary! Sanctuary!" yells Hank.

Bomb Baby

The bomb baby leaps over the thugs' cowering heads, and grabs onto a large elevated brass bust of Pope John Paul II that adorns the churchyard.

Several thugs approach the Rectory. They bang and kick the door. It opens, and Father Gaudi appears. He's old now, but still burly and vigorous. He wears a full-length black cassock and carries the Gospels in one hand, a silver cup filled with consecrated bread in the other. He views the thugs with gentleness. Perhaps he's even a little bored.

Ishida-san approaches in a rage. "Look what that animal did to my baby!"

Across the churchyard the bride can be seen sobbing in the arms of her bridesmaids. Her train is smeared with muddy footprints.

"She's going to bitch in my ear about this for the rest of my life!" cries Ishida-san.

"I'm truly sorry," says Father Gaudi. "But, at the moment, I'm more concerned with your other kids. Or should I call them your slaves?"

"What are you talking about, Priest? Those entertainers have legit work-visas."

Father Gaudi says nothing. Gently but firmly, he elbows Ishida-san aside and begins working his way through the parking lot. He is performing a kind of drive-in ministry, slipping communion to the Filipinas and the transvestites through rolled-down van windows.

Ishida-san follows along, still raging. "How can you charge one-point-five million yen to rent this hall when it's infested?"

Tom Bradley

"It's not a hall. It's the house of God. And you'll have to discuss parish finances with the Bishop. My job is to minister to the foreign community." Father Gaudi inserts a wafer into a pretty Filipina's mouth and says, "The body of Christ."

Crossing herself and munching, the girl replies, "Amen."

"That river-vermin is no member of your precious foreign community," snarls Ishida-san.

"I should say not. If he behaves a little unpleasantly sometimes, it's only because he happened to be in his mother's womb when the Americans pulled their hideous prank on this town. His brain was irradiated."

The bomb baby is sitting cross-legged on top of the brass pope's head. He hoots and blows kisses at a big thug.

"The gamma rays seem to have affected his sense of decorum," says Father Gaudi.

"That's not all that's going to be affected!"

Ishida-san grabs a club from one of his men and stomps a few menacing yards in the bomb baby's direction.

Several Filipinas and transvestites poke their heads out the van windows. The smallest transvestite is a delicate, pretty boy: Audrey Hepburn with a golden-brown complexion. He is too high-strung even in the best circumstances. Today he's on the verge of tears.

"Father! Please don't let them do bad things to B.B.!"

"No danger of that. No matter how loudly Ishida-san screams into their ears, they'll never get close enough to touch our mascot."

Bomb Baby

The pretty Filipina giggles, "He does run fast, doesn't he?"

"He could be a double amputee confined to a broken wheelchair," says Father Gaudi, "and still be safe from the likes of them."

The largest transvestite boldly steps out of the van and reveals himself. He's a strapping youth, well-muscled, with a fine baritone speaking voice, and he looks right at home in his slinky dress, nylons and high heels.

He says, "The Yakuza think B.B's an evil spirit in disguise. Our country may be poor, but even the pygmies on Mount Pinatoba aren't so superstitious."

The bomb baby flips the cigar into the thugs' midst, and they all dive for cover. Several of the foreigners laugh scornfully from the crypt steps.

"God bless the bomb baby's happy soul," says the small transvestite. He pauses, then starts to wail. "And also the soul of my little brother!"

"Mother of God," says Father Gaudi. "What's happened now?"

"They forced him to make the flame dance!"

"There was no time for practicing," says the large transvestite, "because the natives were getting restless. He did his best, Father, but his arms weren't strong enough for the benzine goblets."

"My little brother has burns so horrible, and nobody nurses him!"

As discreetly as possible, so the thug driver won't notice, the large transvestite slips Father Gaudi a piece of paper. "Boys and girls are dying at this address, four or five on a tatami mat."

"You must do something, Father!" says the pretty Filipina.

"I'll be there as soon as I can, I promise you. The body of Christ."

"Amen," sobs the small transvestite.

Ishida-san returns from blustering around the base of the pope's bust. Father Gaudi distracts him from the distraught transvestite by taking his elbow and proceeding to the next vehicle.

Someone passes a charming, racially-mixed baby through a side window. Delighted, Father Gaudi takes it into his arms and carries it to a bench situated just off the parking lot. Ishida-san follows, looking askance at the baby's round eyes and darkish skin. He's affected by the little creature's beauty, in spite of his own racism. He sits down next to the priest and looks out across the cathedral compound.

The foreigners, including Hank and Polly, climb all the way out of the crypt, bringing a couple of guitars for the Filipinas in the vans. Ishida-san listens to their lovely song.

After a moment, he says, "How would your Bishop feel if we renters took our daughters someplace else?"

"Not likely," says Father Gaudi. "Your weddings are pure theater. And this building, hideous as it is, happens to be the most photogenic backdrop in town... With the exception of the Mercedes Benz dealership."

Impressed by Gaudi's nerve, Ishida-san says, "You don't talk like somebody that just got handed one-point-

Bomb Baby

five million yen in cash... Okay. You got me where you want me, Priest... But I have another daughter ripe for marrying. She's my youngest, my favorite."

The bride is throwing a temper tantrum. She screeches and kicks viciously at the shins of the video crew.

"My favorite, by far."

"A second daughter," says Father Gaudi. "Congratulations. Please urge her to attend my Saturday Bible class for non-believers. It's conducted entirely in Hiroshima dialect."

"I've also got friends on the city council. All I need to do is suggest they start regulating river traffic. That's where your precious animal lives, right? On a raft, on the river? Well, the Ministry of Health would just love to burn his raft. No more mud-minnows for supper. He'll be chased up into the hills like a three-legged dog that farts too much."

"The bomb baby doesn't fear mountain heights. That's not why he's chosen the river as his habitat."

"Then what does scare him?"

After a moment's thought, Ishida-san pulls out a solid-gold cigar lighter, a beautiful antique, engraved with dragons, phoenixes and chrysanthemums, which he fingers fondly. Then he adjusts the thing to full flame and waves it in front of Father Gaudi's face like a blow torch.

Father Gaudi casts a protective glance in the bomb baby's direction.

"I should have guessed," says Ishida-san. He's scared of flames, just like all animals."

"I wouldn't blame him if he was, with his pre-natal history."

"No wonder he lives on the water. If he tried pitching camp on the streets with the other bums, he'd be doused with gas and fricasseed on the first night."

"Courtesy of the teenaged bikers. Your fond recruits."

"Sit tight," snickers Ishida-san. "This won't take a second."

He crosses the parking lot, summoning his thugs. On the way, he happens to pass by a rusty, bashed-up Mazda, ineptly parked among the vans. It's difficult to see through the smudged windows, but someone inside is snoring so loudly that the car vibrates on its overloaded, worn-out shocks. Ishida-san forgets what he's doing and stares at this odd sight. But he is distracted by his thugs, who reluctantly gather about him, awaiting his orders. He draws them aside to form a huddle.

Ishida-san sends a little thug to confiscate bouquets from the bewildered bridesmaids.

Polly and Hank, plus a few other foreigners, approach Father Gaudi. "I don't believe this," says Polly. "They're not going to—"

"Of course not," says Father Gaudi. "Too many witnesses. And if the bomb baby comes down, that's no cause for concern, either. Our mascot has a top-secret escape route."

In the Yakuza huddle, the expensive bouquets have been dismantled, the blooms stripped away, and the stems twisted together to make a couple of torches, which Ishida-

Bomb Baby

san has lit. He arms himself with one, and hands the other to a tall thug.

Ishida-san marches to the pope's bust. He waves the fire around the bomb baby's legs and feet. Smoke from the second torch billows up from behind.

Far from being afraid, the bomb baby coos like a dove in fascination. He reaches down and passes his hand through the fire. Without warning, he grabs the torch.

Ishida-san flicks his precious cigar lighter ablaze and tries to set the strange creature's rags on fire. The bomb baby is enchanted. He tosses the torch like a bridal bouquet into the arms of a howling thug, and snatches the beautiful golden thing.

Shrieking in triumph, he conceals the prize in his rags, leaps down among the thugs, scrambles between their cringing legs, vanishes behind the poinsettia bush and exits the sacred precincts, to the tune of the baby abandonment drawer's characteristic squeak.

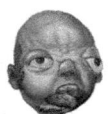

The bomb baby zips down the traffic-jammed street, heading for the river. A few thugs follow, without enthusiasm, hopelessly outpaced.

"Back to the raft, Huckleberry," chuckles Hank.

Polly says, "He didn't even get a chance to come downstairs and pray with us."

Father Gaudi rises to his feet. "We'd better have a conference." With broad arm gestures, he summons the foreigners into the crypt. They all crowd happily down the stairs. Several more Filipinas and transvestites take advantage of the confusion to escape from the vans. Hank rushes to get down the steps ahead of them.

Ishida-san is left to stomp about the compound, cursing and screaming in Hiroshima gutter-dialect.

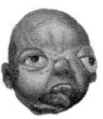

At the front pew, Hank fusses over his bosses' wives as the despised Filipinas come into their presence.

"It's just for a few minutes, I promise. Father has called a kind of powwow. Immediately afterwards these, um, ladies will be on their way back to the parking lot. Okay?"

When he joins Polly in their customary position further back, she asks him, "Do you know the distinguishing characteristic of harem attendants?"

Bomb Baby

"I'm sure you'd volunteer to perform the alterations on me."

Father Gaudi mounts the pulpit. He clears his throat. Everyone shuts up, more or less.

"My friends, we have a problem. A legalistic one yet. After four centuries of wholesome anarchy, I'm afraid that the bomb baby's beloved Ohtagawa River is about to come to the attention of the city council. Today he finally spoiled the wrong wedding."

The voices of various foreigners are heard:

"The cops want to corner B.B. on the streets some night... They'll institutionalize him... Around here, institutionalize means the same as disappear in Argentina... I think I know which institution would take him."

Hank says, "Your hubby's very own university, right, Mrs. Edwine? Their med school's mental health clinic has plenty room for one more. I hear they're bountiful with the thorazine."

Someone says, "Would the bomb baby be willing to dock in one specified place night after night?"

Someone else says, "Do you think he'd be welcomed by his new neighbors at the marina?"

"Getting his raft up to code would take a miracle."

Hank laughs. "Yeah. After he performs that miracle, we'll get the pope to beatify him."

The automotive wives titter at this remark, while some of the more pious foreigners murmur in dismay.

Polly tries to keep things serious. "If the boat mechanics are honest as the car mechanics, being up to code will matter less than paying the inspection fee."

"The professor's wife speaks from experience," says Hank.

"Perhaps," suggests Father Gaudi, "if we open our hearts and our pocketbooks..."

A collection is taken. The pledges and donations pour in from everyone in the crypt, except for the automotive wives. They hesitate to contribute. But then the large transvestite swishes up among them.

"Snap to," says Polly, elbowing Hank. "An underworld figure is invading the harem."

"Drag queens don't count. The ladies simply adore drag queens. Especially this moose. Watch how he handles them."

The large transvestite has perched himself among the wives. "Listen, Lovie-Dovies, if we let the police disappear the bomb baby, who knows what will happen? With no unlucky spirit to scare them away, my handlers might just start coming down here and sharing this bench with you luscious honey-dearies."

An especially stupid wife says, "But your, um, handlers are Japanese. Japanese don't have any religion. Why would they want to invade our chapel?"

"Who can say? Who can say, my little buggy-yummers? You never know. But I can tell you, Sweet-licks, once the Yakuza take over a place, they can be such brutes, such cruel savages. Ooo-ooh!" He flutters his hand on the wives' knees.

"And it helps to look at things from B.B.'s point of view, doesn't it? The poor little fellow. I want you to just

Bomb Baby

try and imagine what it must've been like to bounce around inside somebody's tummy on that morning..."

Lulled by the large transvestite's voice, the automotive wives begin, in spite of themselves, mentally to picture the terrible scenes he describes...

"His mommy tried to jump in the water to bathe her burns, except the atomic blast had parted the river from its bed. Nothing was left behind but glowing mud, not even much good for a poultice. Just a whole bunch of people were overwhelmed and washed away when the boiling Ohtagawa flushed back. The old fishermen's wives say this explains the bomb baby's life-long love affair with the river. Even today he haunts those waters..."

In their minds now, the automotive wives can see the contemporary upstream suburbs of Hiroshima. The river is shallow and lazy, almost lumpy, in the late summer heat. On the flood plain, native families are having picnics and ball games, attempting to enjoy the week's few moments of freedom. Young sons recreate politely with fathers who are strangers to them.

Everybody avoids coming into contact with the polluted water, except for two small children, who know no better than to try to go wading. Their older siblings coax and drag them away, and dry their feet with handkerchiefs, which are promptly discarded into the river.

Tom Bradley

A barely buoyant raft, improvised from bamboo slats tied together with rags, slides from a bank of diesel exhaust. The pilot is none other than the bomb baby. Mothers try to ignore him, and quietly scold their children for staring at his strange face.

The large transvestite says, "Something in B.B. yearns to be washed away with his own beloved townsfolk..."

The bomb baby drifts awhile among turquoise industrial suds. Then he scoops a half-dead fish off the surface and aims it at the sky. A pair of crows appears overhead, croaking loudly. They take turns swooping down to feed on the fish. Occasionally a talon or beak opens a gash in one of the bomb baby's fingers, but this only makes him laugh. The longer he laughs, the more people abandon the flood plain in superstitious fear.

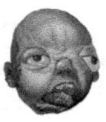

"Now, ladies, I know that our little B.B. makes weird noises from time to time, and is not the most spiffy dresser in all of East Asia. But he's no butch, nipple-tweaking organized crime figure, is he? It's a question of the lesser of two evils, don't you agree, Kissy-poops?"

The wives agree, and come up with a little money.

Hank nearly cries out to Polly, "What did I tell you? Such consummate finesse, such, such—I don't know what to call it!"

"Interpersonal dynamics."

Bomb Baby

"Yeah! If only we could straighten him up. Square him away, just a tad. Get him into a reasonable shade of mascara and some un-laddered nylons. I'm positive there'd be a position waiting for him in our personnel department."

The Nigerian acolyte brings the collection plate to Hank and Polly's pew. Hank looks in and pretends to marvel at the wives' generosity. He casts an adoring, tearful grin in their direction.

The plate is passed into the hands of the only native who worships here, a Japanese amateur archaeologist. He wears a beard and rumpled clothes, very self-consciously in the western academic style. He loads the collection plate with wads of paper money.

"Whoah. Easy," says one of the foreigners. "We're not buying the little monster his own yacht."

Very confidentially, the amateur archaeologist replies, "Soon I'll be able to afford to drop ten times that much. Just ask Ishida-san in about seventy-two hours."

"Don't tell me. You're going to visit his new gambling den and break the bank."

"You could say that. The site he's chosen to build it on has great archeological importance—assuming my research and calculations are correct."

The collection plate is passed to a group of Filipinas. These impoverished girls have no bills, just copper and aluminum coins.

"I will share my money, to help the bomb baby stay free and keep making Ishida-san crazy."

Tom Bradley

Still weeping about his burnt little brother, the small transvestite whimpers, "I hope Ishida-san has twenty fat daughters, so B.B. can be nasty to each of them."

"Come, come," says Father Gaudi. "Let's be charitable. These Yakuza are not free, either."

"Oh?" says the large transvestite. "Who holds Ishida-san in bondage? I don't see any of his fingers missing."

"I don't see patches of his skin scorched away," says the small transvestite."

"Ignorance holds Ishida-san in bondage," says the priest. "And pride compounds that ignorance sevenfold. But he is not completely chained yet. Occasionally I see something else shine through his eyes."

Just as the transvestites' scoffing threatens to get out of hand, the hackneyed wedding march from Lohengrin starts to rumble down on everybody's heads.

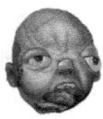

Upstairs, in the cathedral proper, Ishida-san's guests are important civic leaders, ruling party diet men, and pillars of the business community, along with their lovely wives and mistresses. Everyone is arrayed in the correct occidental fashion.

The bridesmaids have tried to dab the bomb baby's footprints away from his daughter's train, but evidence remains, discoloring the lace. Her face is puffed with weeping and a hateful expression.

Bomb Baby

Ishida-san is giving his eldest away, finally, and can't wait to indulge in a cigar. He digs around in his coat for the means to light up, and comes up empty-handed. No gold lighter.

His lieutenant, a reptilian fellow in a rental tux, quickly reaches over and obliges the boss with a lit match. In the flare of the flame, we see that Ishida-san's face is exploding with a borderline-psychotic rage.

In the crypt chapel, the collection plate is passed up to Father Gaudi.

"So, let me see... Ah! My friends, I am pleased to announce that the inspection fee on the bomb baby's raft will be covered."

Cheers are heard from the congregation.

Polly says, "I don't want to spoil the party—"

"Here it comes," mutters Hank.

"—but I have to point something out. The bomb baby likes to grab minnows by hand. That isn't a method the Fishermen's Union will be likely to approve. Somebody should at least show him how to pretend that he can use a line and sinker."

"Mrs. Edwine's observation is, as usual, perfectly astute," says Father Gaudi. "Who will volunteer to teach the bomb baby to pretend to fish?"

All eyes are averted. Nobody wants to do it.

Hank starts smirking. "I just happen to know someone who's perfect for the job. This person's a Ph.D., so he's an expert at pretending to do things."

"Oh, hell," says Polly. "Sorry I mentioned it."

"Since he has a plush university job with unlimited free time, and since he isn't here to defend his interests, I nominate this certain person."

The priest calls for a show of hands. The certain person is elected—with one abstention. Polly tries to decline on his behalf, but she is ignored.

Hank crows like a rooster. "So, we've got ourselves an Official Emissary. I volunteer to be the Chairman of the Angler's Education Committee. That means, Polly dear, that I'll be on him like a cocklebur from now on."

"Who are they talking about?" asks the stupid wife.

"Your guess is as good as mine, Snuggle-bumps," says the large transvestite.

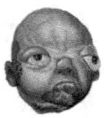

Outside, in the parking lot, some of the thugs are idly gathered around the bashed-up Mazda. To entertain the remaining Filipinas, they unwrap sticks of gum and try to toss the foil wrappers through the car's open window, into the gaping mouth of Polly's husband Sam. He's producing the huge snores that almost deafened Ishida-san.

Wedged in the death seat, Sam Edwine's an enormous-ly tall, heavy-set man, with a flame-orange beard and

24

Bomb Baby

shaggy hair thinning on top. He is dressed in worn-out professorial tweeds, several sizes too small, the leather elbow patches scuffed and hanging by individual threads.

So far, three gum wrappers have made it into Sam's mouth. They adhere to his tongue.

He suddenly awakens. He rolls his eyes with bashful seductiveness, but doesn't bother to spit the wrappers out. In fact, he chews on them awhile, then swallows, neither breaking eye contact with the thugs, nor relaxing his sweet smile.

III.

The Mazda moves slowly through the congestion of a downtown Hiroshima street. A bamboo fishing pole sticks out from the side window, interfering with traffic. Cyclists and pedestrians must duck to avoid decapitation.

Polly is driving. Sam is wadded double in the death seat, a can of lively earthworms squeezed between his knees.

"Why me, for Christ's sake? I've got animals in my lap! Who do they think I am? Saint Fist-Fucking Francis? I don't do church work. I'm not even baptized."

"I tried to decline this honor on your behalf, dear, but the parishioners wouldn't hear of it. You should have seen the Detroit dames. They were thrilled to take on the Hiroshimafia."

"Ouch! God damn it! I can't even look at a fishhook without injuring myself!"

"I don't understand what you're so worried about. How hard can it be to dangle a piece of string in the dinkum wawa?"

"Dinkum wawa? I can't believe you said that. This is a major artery we're talking about, emptying into fathomless deeps."

Bomb Baby

In the hazy distance between two skyscrapers, a slice of the crowded sea can be seen.

"All kinds of awfulness could happen out there on your dinkum wawa."

"You'll be okay. Just use one worm at a time. Sea serpents have much bigger appetites than that."

She turns at a major intersection, opening up a view of a huge traffic jam ahead. Bicycles, cars, taxis, buses and people clog the entrance to Peace Park, site of world-famous Ground Zero.

"Oh, my goodness" says Polly. "Guess what day it is."

"Already?"

"The Golden Anniversary. The Jubilee."

"Call me Mr. Over-Achiever," says Sam, "but I feel like I should spend Sunday filling out applications for jobs in a real country. You know, contributing to our survival."

"You're about to do God's work. That's much more important."

"Hanging out with river riff-raff counts as God's work? Does the Bible tell me so? If I do this, will your God get us off these carcinogenic islands? Will he reach down and magically make me employable in the real world?"

Polly reaches across, puts her hand on his knee and looks very gently into his eyes. "Don't worry, Sammy. I don't mind living here. It's not that nasty a country. You're a perfectly good provider."

"The big P. What a ridiculous word."

"The whole point, Dear, is this: today you will have a chance to know the inner contentment that comes from doing good works. As the Bible says: *Whatsoever you do to the least of my brothers you do unto me.*"

She pulls up to the curb, and whispers in his vast ear, "We'll get home someday."

They exchange a long look.

"Don't let him keep you out all night. There's squid tentacle sushi for supper."

The car lurches three feet into space with Sam's exit.

Just as the car is pulling away from the entrance to Peace Park, Sam remembers to reach in and grab the bamboo pole and can of worms. He shouts, "Okay! I guess I'll be a nice guy, just this one time, and show the bomb baby how to fool the Fishermen's Union!"

Towering over the crowd of international peace lovers, who have come to commemorate A-Bomb Day, Sam mutters to himself, "Hmm. The joy of doing good works. Never thought of that. Sounds pretty wild. I'll try anything once."

He drops the fishing stuff, shoots his cuffs, sucks up his gut and tucks in his shirt, which comes untucked again when he exhales. He lunges off into the mob.

He comes back, on second thought, gathers up the pole and worms, then lunges back into the mob—

But he's forced to skid to a halt, because some high school students cross his path. Even on this hot August Sunday they're buttoned into stifling woolen uniforms and loaded down with book-stuffed satchels.

"Ah!" says Sam. "Suffer the little children to come unto me. Study hard, babies, and maybe someday you'll be my disciples at the big important university!"

Bomb Baby

They don't even glance at him. Distracted by neither the giant American nor the holiday celebration, the high school students move in joyless lockstep, like haggard robots, down the block. Sam watches them in amazement as they vanish into a weekend cram school. Over the door is a garish sign that reads—

LET US LEARNING THE ENGLISH!

The Mayor of Hiroshima stands on a raised dais in the middle of the park. He's a diminutive codger with a Hirohito-Hitler mustache. All dressed up for the big Jubilee, he wears white gloves, a silk ribbon sash, and a blood-colored carnation which obscures almost the entire front of his boy-sized morning coat. He somberly releases clouds of diseased doves from chrome-plated cages.

Directly upon release, the poor animals, which have plastic olive branches stapled symbolically to their upper beaks, skid straight into the grass like overloaded sailplanes. They're trampled to grease spots by stampeding International Peace Lovers.

By far the most conspicuous member of the motley multitude is Sam Edwine. On his face is an expression of religious ecstasy, because he's doing God's good work, bringing comfort and joy to the heathen.

Tom Bradley

He dances little jigs, nudging everybody aside with his gyrating pelvis. He leaps into the air with all the bashful-eyed grace of the hippo ballerinas in Disney's *Fantasia*. He swings the bamboo fishing pole around like a fairy god-mother's wand, and sprinkles worms from the can like banana peels in everyone's path.

Small schoolchildren on a field trip break ranks and scatter in terror at Sam's approach. Their teacher shrieks, "Get back in line, or the big devil will eat you up!"

Somewhat farther along the path, standing at full attention among barbecued cuttlefish booths, is a platoon of male college cheerleaders, Sam's students. These junior fascists are dressed in WWII-style military uniforms of dark-blue wool. They're rallied under giant radiating-sun flags and banners emblazoned with reversed and righted swastikas. Their boom-box blares martial music and racist propaganda. A couple of these cheerleaders hold up a big placard which reads, in both Japanese and English—

WE ARE A DIVINE NATION
WITH THE EMPEROR AT OUR CENTER!

One bulldog-like cheerleader screams into a megaphone, "Japan is a tiny rice paddy! America is a treeless peak! Flood control is paramount!"

Everyone is terrified of these fanatical boys—everyone except Sam, of course. He barges through their ranks.

Among the cheerleaders is a thin boy with glasses, who looks frazzled. He is Sam's most nervous student. Sam

Bomb Baby

shouts at him, "Why aren't you at home studying your English? It's a required course, you know!"

The nervous student almost faints from embarrassment. He gobbles some pharmaceutical amphetamines from a little prescription bottle. It looks like he's got quite a habit.

Feeling really holy now, Sam prances further into the A-Bomb Golden Anniversary Celebration, heading toward Ground Zero.

Deep in the park, tucked behind a row of ornamental azalea bushes, is a shanty town where some of Hiroshima's bums live in washing machine cartons. A few of them are the bomb baby's exact age, and are deformed or brain-damaged because they were exposed to the A-bomb's radiation inside their mothers' wombs.

A proud platoon of Hiroshima city cops comes marching up in full Jubilee regalia: white gloves and gaiters, silken shoulder braids, golden epaulettes, and so on. They've come to roust the bums.

Sam dances onto the scene, his whole head aglow with divine inspiration. A few bums break away and hobble over to greet him, their old pal. They stand on tiptoe, stroke his beard, and babble like pleased babies.

Tom Bradley

Sam interposes his vast body between them and the clutching claws of the police. He's getting joy from doing good works.

"Whatever you pricks do to my little brothers, you do to me! Why not let them join the party? This is their home! These cats are Ground Zero's regular and rightful residents!"

He pauses to slap a white-gloved hand from a grimy Adam's apple.

"Why are you doing this? To prettify this dump? For the benefit of today's visitors? Are you kidding? Have you even bothered to look at your foreign guests?"

Sam calls the cops' attention to the throng of international peace lovers, liberals to an individual.

"It would tickle them pink to be spare-changed by genuine native hoboes! It's my fascist students you should be giving the bum's rush to! They're the ones jeopardizing municipal tourist revenue!"

The cops eventually recover from their shock and start looking angry. So Sam gets scared and decides to move off. He looks pretty sheepish at first, but gradually recovers his divine inspiration. Sam's prancing again by the time the crowd swallows him up.

The cops are left to do their job. Wielding spotless ivory dress-truncheons, they bust several heads, smash up the shanty town, and hustle the poor guys off.

Only one little cardboard bungalow remains standing.

Bomb Baby

Inside, a deformed bum squats on his haunches, staring in puzzlement at a needle jammed deep in his arm. His blood is being harvested by a small, twitchy *Bangladeshi* named Mamoon.

Dressed in a white lab coat several sizes too big, Mamoon is an assistant radiation effects researcher. He comes equipped with a little black bag such as doctors once used for house calls. The bag clinks with glass vials and hypodermic syringes.

He peeks out a hole in the cardboard wall to see if the cops are gone.

Wearing a look of saintly ecstasy, Sam is doing the Boogaloo at the epicenter.

Mamoon catches up and tugs on his coattails. Under the radiation effects researcher's arm is a well-stuffed Manila envelope.

"Why, bless my wholesome soul," bellows Sam. "If it's not the Pakistani radioactivity guy."

"Oh, please, Dr. Edwine. Must we go through this every time? It's the Bangladeshi radioactivity guy."

Tom Bradley

"Who said you could come down from the Mountain of Slow Death?" asks Sam, gesturing with a thumb toward Mount Hijiyama, which hulks in the polluted distance.

The Radiation Research Foundation can be seen in the middle of an acid rain-ravaged bamboo grove at the summit. It's a squalid and sinister place, housed in several large dilapidated WWII-vintage Quonset huts.

"Did you bring your locally famous boss, the illustrious Bruiser?"

"My supervisor's name happens to be Valentina. Nobody but you calls her the Bruiser. And she rarely leaves her lab."

"That makes you the only sane resident of Hiroshima within five blocks of this shindig. Besides me, of course... And I, if you must know, happen to be on a divine mission."

"I have a delivery to make on the far side of the park."

"A delivery, eh, Mamoon? And a pick-up, too, I'll just bet. Sucking on radioactive arteries like a bumblebee on flowers."

Sam throws down his fishing tackle and snatches the Manila envelope. Ignoring Mamoon's whimpers of protest, he rips it open and examines the contents. It's a sheaf of illustrations xeroxed from medical textbooks: gory post-mortem photos of botched thoracic and brain surgery.

"Damn! Some kind of ugsome!"

"Such pictures make your bomb baby's face light up."

"You gene-jammers cherish B.B., don't you? He's the most exquisitely futuristic mutant this glamorous town has to offer. But you'll never be able to probe his secrets."

Bomb Baby

"Oh, I wouldn't be so sure about that. He's willing to hold still for three minutes or so, in exchange for a stack of postmortems, like those you're holding in your hand."

"Three minutes?" Sam rolls up the pictures and sticks them in his pocket. "That's barely long enough to get a syringe unwrapped and his stringy biceps tied off. How frustrating for you... Could you hold this for a second?"

He gathers the fishing stuff back up and shoves it into Mamoon's hands, causing him to drop his black bag. The glass vials inside break and dozens of samples slosh out, soaking Ground Zero with mutant blood.

Then Sam moves in on Mamoon, chasing him in circles. Sam reaches down, digs his fingers into the folds of the unfortunate Bangladeshi's lab coat, and tickles him without a hint of mercy. Mamoon cringes in an agony of embarrassment. He's so flustered, it doesn't occur to him to drop the pole and worms and defend himself. He can only hold his elbows tight against his sides.

Several dozen assorted lovers of international harmony gather to stare, unsure as to how they should react to this sight.

"Please, Dr. Edwine! In my culture, men don't touch so readily!"

"Oh, gee. I didn't know that. I thought this was normal behavior on the subcontinent. I guess I'd better stop doing this, huh? Huh?"

Sam stops when he feels like it.

Shakily composing himself, Mamoon mutters, "It's time I kept my appointment with our little friend. The pictures, please."

"Oh. I almost forgot." He peeks again at the postmortems. "I've got to hand it to you gamma ghouls. Till now he only came ashore to spoil bourgeois weddings."

"What's your secret reason for befriending such a specimen, Dr. Edwine? Somehow I can't believe you're running a divine errand for the Christians, or even for your wife."

"My wife? Did you mention my wife, Moony? Don't talk to me about being hen-pecked. You, who dance attendance on the Bruiser for a living."

"Her name happens to be—"

"I never understood why your country needs radiation researchers in the first place."

"We don't want to be caught unprepared for the only disaster that hasn't befallen us yet."

"How prudent of you."

Mamoon is trying to calculate an efficient way to hold the fishing pole and can of worms, from which several specimens are escaping. They crawl up the white sleeve of his lab coat, leaving gray trails. He fails to notice them.

"Besides," he says, "Valentina gives me free run of the pharmacology lab on Sundays, to do my—" (pausing and leering) "—*private research*, so to speak."

"Don't tell me about whatever designer poisons you're cooking up. As a professor at Boom Town U., I'm expected to behave myself. And I only associate with guys who do likewise."

"Then take my advice and shun your wife's pewmate."

Bomb Baby

"Polly has several pew-mates. Are we talking about a first-, second- or third-worlder?"

"We're talking about Hank."

"Oh, sure. Hank's a real wild man, with his perfect ponytail. A creative artist, a savage. Watch out!"

A worm has made it all the way up to Mamoon's lapel. Sam eyes it and tries not to laugh. He has to look away. He squints through the smog at the Radiation Research Foundation.

"Do you really expect that dump to stay standing for 200 years?"

"That's how many generations of natives we need to study. They don't call it *long-term genetic damage* for nothing. In the meantime, Dr. Edwine, if you'd be so kind as to allow Valentina and me to do our work—"

Mamoon looks down at his little black bag, which lies in a pool of gore on the ground. He pokes it sadly with the fishing pole, causing the shattered paraphernalia inside to clink.

"—maybe we can unearth a few really spectacular mutations here and now. We could get some serious funding for a change. Spacious labs, air conditioning, a proper commissary with a vegetarian menu."

"Altruist."

"Please give me the pictures back."

"Nope. Sorry. This is one bloodletting I can prevent. Today you're just going to have to report back to the Bruiser empty-handed. Oh, you're in for such a spanking, Moony. Cruisin' for a bruisin'... Are you done playing with Double B.'s toys yet?"

Tom Bradley

Sam snatches the fishing gear and hulks off into the crowd, Mamoon's postmortems poking from his pocket.

The Bangladeshi shouts after him, "Don't forget to tell your bomb baby where the pictures came from! Please? Dr. Edwine? Sir?" (lowering his voice) "Thieving infidel dog, Sir? Filthy American imperialist bully bastard swine. Sir?"

Mamoon stomps off in the direction of Mount Hijiyama. His little black bag clinks as he goes. He sounds like a midget milkman.

The Radiation Research Foundation is a dreary, dank, under funded institution, olive-drab. The furnishings and filing cabinets look like leftovers from the days of General MacArthur. Even the various international scientists exhibit a certain mid-1940's sense of style as they slink up and down the gloomy corridors.

Ray Conniff's rendition of "Red Roses for a Blue Lady" hisses through cheap monaural speakers nailed to the cobwebby walls. This is intended to soothe the nerves of the radiation victims who loiter listlessly outside the laboratories, waiting their turn to get poked and prodded. They have been dragged here weekly for the past half-century, for liver biopsies, blood tests and tissue samples.

Valentina is in her lab. She's a fleshy and more-or-less voluptuous citizen of the former Soviet Union. Under her

Bomb Baby

lab coat she has big protuberant middle-aged breasts and wide hips. She busily flips the air bubbles out of a syringe.

An aging radiation victim hovers over his retarded sister, who is strapped down on a gurney. She squirms and hoots as he tries to calm her with a soft folk song, gently tapping time on her shoulder.

Oblivious to the retarded sister's cries, Valentina draws what seems like an excessive amount of blood. She labels the vial, and places it on the shelf among countless other vials, many of them labeled "B.B."

Mamoon shows up and quietly tries to stow his little black bag under a table, but its clinking catches Valentina's attention.

"No, no," she growls. "You show me."

Trembling, Mamoon empties the bag on the table. He has no blood samples to show, only scabby glass splinters.

"So, you come up dry, little man? You dare penetrate my personal space empty-handed?"

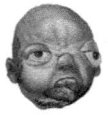

At the riverbank border of Peace Park, the bomb baby's frayed mooring line is lassoed around a utility pole. It straggles over the azalea bushes on the levee, and droops down through the mud to the bomb baby's raft, which looks like a load of trash and wood scraps bound for a bonfire upstream.

Tom Bradley

Sam crashes through the azaleas and proudly holds up his three gifts: the can of worms, the bamboo fishing pole, and the sheaf of stolen postmortems.

The bomb baby dashes up the embankment and makes a beeline for the pictures. He peers at them, making compassionate sounds in the base of his throat. He strokes the pages, puts a tragic look on his face, and holds them up for Sam to share.

"What's-his-name wasn't kidding," says Sam. "You really do like splatter-shots, don't you? Well, I'm delighted to be the one who was thoughtful enough to xerox them for you. They come from me. From Sam."

He writes those last two words on the envelope and tries to persuade the bomb baby to look at them and repeat them.

"F-R-O-M S-A-M. Not the little man in the white coat who comes off the dark mountain. Stay away from him. He's so mean and dangerous..."

Mamoon is ashamed to look in his supervisor's eyes. He's like a little schoolboy confessing to Mommy that the bullies stole his lunch money. He flinches, expecting to be cuffed on the side of the head.

"Where are the pictures?" barks Valentina. "You gave them to the moron and got nothing in return?"

Bomb Baby

Sam follows the bomb baby down into his floating home. The raft's superstructure has been improvised from cardboard boxes and discarded tatami mats, rescued from mulch piles and slapped on the deck. It's a shadowy, smoky enclosure, with some chinks in the makeshift walls that let in a little light and air.

Having scooped a handful of mud off the bank before entering, the bomb baby is pasting up his new gory xeroxes.

Mamoon whines, "The big American took them away from me."

In the corner of the bomb baby's living space, Ishida-san's lovely golden cigar lighter has been enshrined on a beer crate, surrounded by hundreds of burning jasmine joss sticks.

Tom Bradley

"This place looks just like my bedroom back in high school," says Sam. "Same basic style of decor. Smells like it, too. Where'd you get all the hip incense?"

As if in reply, the bomb baby squats before his shrine and makes the sign of the cross. He begins to yowl, "Bod-dy Chris'! Blood-dy Chri-i-is'!"

"Oh, you naughty boy! You snitched it from the sacristy, didn't you? Terrible little rapscallion, looting the sanctuary."

Sam picks up a joss stick, which burns his fingers. He drops it on the deck. It bounces against several small plastic bags of yellowish crystalline powder stacked in a suspiciously neat pyramid against the wall.

With a contemptuous grunt, Valentina turns her back on Mamoon.

He eventually gathers his nerve back, and sidles up to a stainless steel tray full of medical paraphernalia and blood-splotched cotton squares. They look like piles of tiny rising-sun flags. Mamoon snatches a couple ampules of something that looks like egg nog.

Valentina stands nearby, watching his every move through the corner of one eye, meanwhile testing the edge of a scalpel on her thumb.

Mamoon sneaks out of the room. Valentina watches him go, and smiles fondly at his naughtiness. Then she

Bomb Baby

closes in again on the retarded sister, this time for a hefty tissue sample.

In the pharmacology lab Mamoon spasms among pyrex beakers and Bunsen burners. He mixes the contents of the stolen ampules with other noxious-looking materials. He pulls a bowl of yellowish crystalline powder from a microwave oven, and begins spooning the illegal-looking stuff into small plastic bags, for retail distribution. It's the same stuff we've already seen on the raft.

Puzzled, Sam takes out his own cigarette lighter to help him see the stack of little bags more clearly through the gloom. By the light of the flame, we see that the bomb baby's walls are completely papered over with Mamoon's medical textbook illustrations. Sam surveys this gallery of death in appalled amazement.

Seated on a lab stool near Mamoon is Hank, the self-proclaimed Chairman of the Angler's Education Committee. He's flipping through a pile of photographs of Hiroshima's homeless people. He selects one in particular to wave gleefully in Mamoon's face.

Taken aback, Mamoon gasps, "Please tell me you're not—"

"It's *interesting*," laughs Hank. "We're employing Pavlovian means, or whatever that's called."

The photo is of the bomb baby on his raft.

The bomb baby is trying to snatch Sam's cigarette lighter.

"What are you," says Sam, "a man or a magpie? Don't be so greedy. It's just a disposable. See? Not even shiny."

The bomb baby collapses into a dejected heap and whimpers.

"Okay, okay. Here."

Sam's attention has been distracted from the bags. He follows the bomb baby out onto the deck and allows him a few minutes to frolic in the smoggy sunshine with his new toy.

"Okay, now, before we begin our first fishing lesson, allow me to explain why it would be desirable to learn to hold this bamboo pole in such and such a way—"

But the student is not listening. He squats and begins to scratch the mud away from certain flat stones on the riverbank, revealing the scorched silhouettes of carp skeletons in terminal agony.

Bomb Baby

"I'll be damned!" marvels Sam. "X-rays! So this must be the place where the river got blasted away. Is this where your poor neighbors fell for the old Red Sea ruse?"

On the opposite bank, street urchins are gathering and cat-calling. They try to torment the bomb baby by pitching one-yen pieces into the water like tiny skipping stones, and daring him to dive for them. Working-class grown-ups join in on the fun. Copper fives and tens come sailing across.

Sam yells, "Why are you worthless lowbrows trying to tease him?"

"Call it a protest against the consumption tax!"

"Yeah! If all our loose change is in the hands of idiots, there's no way the government can scrape another three percent of the flesh off our bones!"

With a bribe of a handful of silver from Sam, the bomb baby is able to withstand the temptation. So the street urchins and the grownups shift tactics. They tear pages from a luridly sadomasochistic comic book, wad them up, and toss them into the river.

"If money doesn't get a plunge out of the monkey, the manga never fail! He loves pictures of pain!"

Finally seduced, the bomb baby wades out into the water.

"Come back to the raft again, Huck-honey!" cries Sam.

Several hours later, they haven't moved an inch. The fishing pole lies idle in the mud; the worms have escaped from the can; and Sam sits on the deck with his elbows on his knees, his head cradled dejectedly in his hands. Almost the entire afternoon has passed without a single line being cast.

On a jetty not far upriver a banner can be seen unfurling. It reads:

ANNUAL LANTERN-FLOATING CEREMONY

Dignitaries of the liberal persuasion from all over the world are showing up with their personal video crews and retinues of toadies and press agents. They hold silent prayer vigils and offer photo opportunities. Squatting on the bunting-festooned jetty, they launch lit candles in tiny, colorful floating lanterns, in order to secure a lasting world peace. A news crew from a local TV station captures everything.

The sound man asks, "Wouldn't the lanterns be more effective if they were launched after dark?"

"Sure," replies the cameraman. "But then we couldn't get such excellent shots of these foreigners' solemn profiles. Aren't their noses wonderful?"

The floating lanterns blunder a few feet downstream into the gathering gloom, and get mired in a miniature doldrum on the far bank. One lantern capsizes, setting the oily surface of this puddle faintly, bluishly ablaze.

The bomb baby appears from nowhere, delightedly vocalizes, and leaps in to bathe himself in fire. The dignita-

Bomb Baby

ries upstream shy back from the jetty when they hear him babbling in the shadows.

"B.B. tempura!" cries Sam, who lounges on the deck. "Does it bring back memories? Fifty years ago today, was your mommy's womb-water boiling like that? I think I'm beginning to understand what my wife's pew-mates see in you, my pal."

The bomb baby splashes awhile happily. But then his skewed eyes look out across the river. Hundreds of flickering flames are descending upon him, more floating lanterns. This is too much fire even for a bomb baby. He makes panicky sounds in the base of his throat and clambers up the embankment to hide in the bulrushes.

"Oh, I forgot," says Sam. This is your annual night to sleep ashore, isn't it?"

The bomb baby responds only with whimpers.

"Relax, will you? I never understood why you get so upset every year. All we have to do is position ourselves upstream. I'll show you. Let's row awhile, toward my place, and the fire will go away from us."

But the bomb baby hesitates to come out.

"It must be like a recurring nightmare for you. This one night keeps rolling around every year, when your home seems to break out in flames. But you have to eat a little supper before bedtime. Otherwise your tummy might growl and give you bad dreams about unlucky ghosts and devils. Come back to the raft again. Let's catch us a school of juicy, nutritious rainbow trout before pitching camp. That's why God sent me here with this tackle and trim."

Tom Bradley

The bomb baby minces through the mud on cringing tiptoes and climbs aboard, rubbing his belly and making hand-to-mouth eating motions. He pitches the fishing pole like a javelin deep into the shadows.

Together, they shove off from Peace Park. In the deepening evening light they navigate slowly up the lazy river, toward Hiroshima's suburbs.

There's no regulation at all on this water, no right of way, not even an agreed-upon side to navigate on. The wakes of the various craft are tangled together like strands of poorly braided hair.

In the dusk-light, further upstream, the bomb baby scavenges for his supper, with Sam's assistance. He pokes among the bulrushes for shoreside carrion. He noses into a few marina dumpsters.

Superstitious night fishermen occasionally float by and toss him a cold rice ball or two, to propitiate this unlucky spirit. They do double takes at the big foreigner on board. Sometimes the fishermen offer to tow the raft upstream a

Bomb Baby

little way. The bomb baby casts them his mooring line and the raft is pulled slowly along. At these times he smiles and croons like an angel in heaven. He lies on his belly and dangles his hand in the water.

Sam watches the bomb baby's face in fascination. Maybe even in awe.

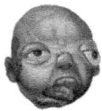

At a riverside construction site, Ishida-san's new gambling den is taking shape. A big billboard on the roof reads—

HOME OF THE BRAVE
GRAND OPENING SOON!

As furtively as possible, the Japanese amateur archaeologist scales a clanking chain link fence at the periphery. He creeps about in the shadows, pries back a couple slabs of reinforced concrete and snoops among the weeds. He hears the raft being rowed up the river. It heaves into sight, just off the near bank.

The bomb baby, at the oar, notices the trespasser first. Babbling and tugging on Sam's coattails, he makes shoveling motions and happily points at the archaeologist.

Sam looks up, waves, and shrieks, "Yoo-hoo! Digger man! Why on earth are you trespassing on the bloodthirsty mobster's property? Do you have a death wish?"

Tom Bradley

The bomb baby imitates Sam. "Igger-bah! Obberty! Bish?"

The archaeologist panics. He holds a finger to his lips and makes frantic "shhhhh!" sounds. He dives into the weeds and crawls away before Ishida-San or one of the thugs can see him.

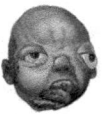

Ishida-san himself is personally overseeing the construction work, an unlit cigar clenched between his lips. He is proudly showing the place to two American auto executives, Hank's bosses, one skinny and one fat. Dressed in expensive business suits, they look like potential investors. Hank hovers between them and Ishida-san, serving as interpreter.

Sam and the bomb baby row slowly by, like Huck Finn and Jim.

"Hank! Ha-a-a-ankie! Hankums! Hoo-hoo! Fellatio is a lot easier if you get down on your knees!"

Hank pretends the crazy goon on the river is screaming at someone else by that name. Ishida-san does a slow burn. He stares at the raft and its two strange occupants, particularly the bomb baby, who's sucking on his solid-gold cigar lighter.

Sam stares right back at the crime boss and, ever so slowly, flips the bird. He doesn't break eye-contact or lower his middle finger till they row out of sight.

Bomb Baby

Further upstream, the bomb baby starts getting a bit hungry for dessert. He rubs his belly. So they run the raft aground in the shallows. He hesitates. Then, with a gentle shove from Sam, he submerges himself and commences cupping up double handfuls of the sluggish minnows.

"See?" says Sam. "This night's no different from any other."

Sam lies on his belly on the deck, his chin comfortably cradled in the palms of his hands.

"To hell with it. Right, buddy? To hell with the Fishermen's Union. To hell with Ishida-san and his goons and his pet councilmen. To hell with the churchy crowd and the gamma ghouls. To hell with everybody except us little ones. Eat hardy, B.B., and God bless your half-hatched self."

IV.

Later that evening, in Hiroshima Cathedral's organ loft, the two American Auto Executives have taken up uncomfortable positions in the Asiatic-sized choir stalls. They've brought their underling Hank along. He stands. Father Gaudi has seated himself on the organ bench.

"So," says the priest, "we have a little boycott brewing, do we?"

The skinny auto executive replies, "Our wives don't enjoy sharing their place of worship with hardened criminals."

"Oh, I see. It's the hardened ones they don't like. Well, those particular criminals have voluntarily confined themselves to the parking lot."

"So far. But what if the pimps decide to come in some Sunday? It's bad enough that our wives have to risk catching AIDS from sharing the communion cup with whores."

"Excuse me," says Father Gaudi, "but I don't like the way your upper lip curled when you said pimps and whores. In our efforts to survive, we all contribute to the defilement of this world, don't we?" He gestures across the loft railing at the interior of the cathedral. Automotive smog fills even this indoor space.

Bomb Baby

"Great," grunts the fat auto executive. "A green priest. That's all we need."

"Everybody, except your wives, heartily welcomes the Filipinas to church each week. And nobody—again with the exception of your lovely wives—has objected to learning The Lord's Prayer in Tagalog."

"A birds-and-bees type. Never read the verse about being fruitful and subduing the god-damned earth."

"Most of the parishioners don't get a chance to subdue anything. They're too busy being subdued themselves by men like you."

"A god-damned lefty to boot! Where'd you say you're from?"

Proudly, Father Gaudi replies, "I am Catalonian."

"Where's that? Central America, right? What are you, one of those Liberation Theologians?"

The skinny auto executive starts doing a stereotype Mexican accent. "Padre no been home to the hacienda for long, long time. Not since before us gringos nuked Boom Town."

Ignoring that bit of stupidity, Father Gaudi rises to his feet. "I can tell you that they are simmering inside, many members of our congregation. They're boiling with outrage against the feudal-minded culture in which they find themselves submerged every day of their exiled lives—"

"Every day except Sunday. Or at least those Sundays when no gangster weddings are scheduled overhead."

"Oh, yeah," says the fat auto executive. "I heard about those high-tone bashes. No wonder the great Gaudi can afford to turn his nose up at our wives' offerings. He's got Nip Mafiosos for sugar daddies."

But the priest is gaining momentum. "As for the pimps, as you call them: is it possible to name anybody in greater need of grace than those men? Every day of my life I pray that they may overcome their superstitious fears and descend the steps; that they may sit in our little chapel and listen to us sing and watch how we pray."

He looms over the Americans.

"And, after I beseech God to provide this small miracle, sometimes I even remember to ask that you gentlemen, and your associates, will follow on the pimps' heels, your hats in your hands, your eyes downcast in utter humility!"

Overwhelmed, but loath to show it, the skinny auto executive mutters, "Maybe we should make an appointment with the Bishop."

The Americans retreat from the loft. Hank hangs back long enough to flip a delighted thumbs-up, to which the priest does not respond.

In the night shadows at the cathedral's side gate, two black stretch limousines are waiting. The first contains Ishida-san, who gets out, greets the two auto executives, and directs them to the second limo.

Bomb Baby

Hank rushes ahead and struggles with a thug chauffeur for the privilege of opening the door for his bosses. He succeeds, and reveals a golden-eyed girl and another bewildered pubescent Filipina, huddled and quaking in the vast back seat. Before the auto executives close in on them, they crane their necks to get a glimpse of God's house.

As he climbs in, the fat auto executive starts breathing hard. "You ladies smell pretty tonight. Clean as a whistle. Just like a breath of fresh air, after that church. Stank like bent tacos in there."

When he lays hands on the golden-eyed girl, she screams in revulsion, shoves him away, and bolts out the door. She pushes past Ishida-san, who is waiting on the sidewalk, according to the cordial Japanese custom, ready to wave and bow until the honored patrons drive out of sight.

His face inscrutable, Ishida-san gives a nod of the head to a fleet-footed thug riding shotgun in the Americans' limo. This human cheetah chases the golden-eyed girl about half a block, and stops her with a flying tackle. She screams again as her beautiful face scrubs into broken glass and gravel in the gutter.

"Looks like that one's out of commission for the night," says the skinny auto executive. "We're going to have to double up now. I hope this means we get a fifty-percent discount."

Ishida-san pretends not to hear that. He walks into the cathedral's side gate.

Tom Bradley

The lieutenant makes sure the interior of the cathedral is secure before his boss enters. Ishida-san comes in by the chancel door. He climbs the spiral staircase to the organ loft, and seats himself next to Gaudi on the organ bench. No greetings are exchanged. The mood is oddly intimate. Ishida-san has brought a photo of his younger daughter.

"I'm sure you know, Priest, how hard it is to marry off Hiroshima girls. Genetic damage and so forth—"

"You are starting to cut into my free time, Ishida-san."

"—but I managed to find her a real stand-up guy. Unlike her big sister, this girl is life to me. She's my beautiful princess. All her classmates had authentic weddings. Why should she be left out?"

"Let's get to the point, shall we? the bomb baby crawls over the embankment for one reason only. He has made a lifetime hobby of spoiling weddings in this place. Yours was far from the first. Over the past generation he has infuriated every rich family in town at least once."

"Do you blame us for getting mad? That animal ruins the authentic mood of this hall—"

As the crime boss speaks, he gestures over the organ loft rail at the concrete walls, the cheap abstract-expressionist stained glass, the various inept depictions of Christ on the cross, etc.

"This stuff really impresses us *Nihonjin*. The kids today are nuts about authentic weddings. My beautiful princess has got to have one. You better cure your mascot of his bad habits before the time comes, or else."

"Or else what?"

Ishida-san pretends not to hear the question. "Have you noticed how kids these days got no religion, no respect the beliefs of their elders? Teenaged bikers aren't nearly as finicky as my men about mixing it up with an evil spirit."

"Oh, come now, Mr. Ishida. A beating will have no effect on his behavior. This little one's mind can't associate causes with effects. You know that as well as I. His consciousness floats like an empty sushi box in a river. He's almost as bad as an American."

"I don't sympathize with that kind of mental laziness. I'm a businessman, the hardest worker in this workaholic town."

"Yes, and thanks to your hard work, the city council will soon take the bomb baby's raft away. So he'll probably start attending receptions and rehearsals as well."

Ishida-san is filled with rage. He forces himself to stay calm. "Do you know where this animal spends his nights?"

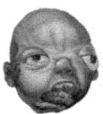

At a riverside driving range, hundreds of Japanese salarymen are practicing golf shots from three tiers. Their drives almost never make it to the far net, where the bomb baby has established his secret campsite.

He is bedding down for the night, wrapping himself in the lower billows and seams of the green net. He vanishes into greenness.

The raft is moored to the nearby bushes. Sam lies flat on his back on the deck, fiddling with the bomb baby's crooked oar, waving it through the air like Toscanini's baton.

Directly across the Ohtagawa is a mammoth apartment building with purple plastic balconies. Polly stands on a sixth-floor balcony. She holds out into space a large piece of sushi. It features a dollop of chartreuse horseradish peeking out from under a generous chunk of purple squid tentacle.

She calls, into the distance, "Suppertime, Sammy!"

V.

Next day, in Hiroshima's wealthy residential district, the hillside houses are looking splendid, if scaled down by American standards. We glimpse emerald-green back gardens between white stone walls. From the windows of adolescents' bedrooms, the most antisocial rock music can be heard—but it's turned down to a furtive whisper.

A city bus pulls up and expels several Filipina domestic servants, arriving for work in the surrounding homes. They are not young or attractive enough to be forced into prostitution like their sisters. But their exhausted appearance makes it clear that they're being exploited in other ways.

Mamoon, the radiation effects researcher, follows these poor women off the bus. He totes his clinking black bag.

Following on his heels is a fat middle-aged Filipina named Imelda. She looks and acts a lot like Ferdinand Marcos' well-shod widow. She wears a vulgarly sequined dress, the same shade of pale turquoise which swathes figurines of the Virgin Mary in Catholic churches. Her feet are pinched into the kind of spike heels favored by streetwalkers. Imelda can barely lumber off the bus, so Mamoon is forced to hold her elbow, much to his distaste.

Tom Bradley

Slouching by are some of the high school students who passed Peace Park on their way to the cram school. Buttoned up in their woolen uniforms, burdened with enormous book bags, they look far too haggard and cynical for their tender age. They're coming up the hill, from the direction of the river.

Suppressing a wicked smile, Imelda remarks, "Poor dears. They're allowed so little pleasure in their lives."

A few of the high school students duck behind a bush for several seconds. They come out again, wiping their noses and looking much more chipper. Mamoon watches them approvingly. Then he leads Imelda down the incline, in the direction the teens came from.

On the Ohtagawa riverbank, Mamoon and Imelda sneak into a bamboo grove, where the raft has been run aground in the mud. The bomb baby is squatting on the deck, and seems to be waiting for them. Mamoon pulls out a fresh batch of gory pictures and waves them in his face, like a bone for a spaniel. The bomb baby is pleased, and grabs the gift.

In a grotesque caricature of gallantry, he offers his elbow to Imelda. She looks like she'd rather handle worms, but accepts the offer. The three of them go inside the raft's superstructure, Imelda tiptoeing unsteadily. Mamoon tries

Bomb Baby

to come into contact with as little as possible. Unlike Sam, he is disgusted by the bomb baby's home.

After a few minutes Mamoon comes out on deck, alone. He is placing wads of banknotes and vials of fresh ruby-red blood into his black bag.

Imelda soon follows, wiping sticky whitish moisture from her face and looking as though she needs to barf. Snatching at the money, she hisses, "Some of that belongs to me."

A few Sundays later, the Yakuza's office is quite busy. It's a two-story hub of organized crime, located blatantly in a lower-middle-class residential neighborhood.

A patrol car makes a U-turn rather than pass by this building, as dozens of thugs brazenly punch in and out with bags full of drug money and crates of handguns. Ishida-san has the cops so firmly in his pocket that discretion is not necessary.

Some housewives are gathered around a laundry line next door. One of them almost shouts, "This street is getting very busy lately, isn't it, ladies?"

The others all concur, very loudly. Meanwhile their cowardly husbands slink off to the driving range with golf bags, eyes fearfully averted from the thugs.

Father Gaudi, dressed in his full-length black cassock, approaches the front door. He gently confronts the sentry, who's big and tough, but reluctant to face the old priest. Father Gaudi touches his arm. After a silent moment, the sentry's eyes fill with tears, and he stands aside.

In a back room, half a dozen Filipinas and transvestites are crowded on the floor. All of them are suffering terribly from the injuries and diseases associated with the sick sex which native customers force them to perform.

Father Gaudi walks in and takes a look around. He does a double take at a shadowy figure propped in the corner, which looks and sounds just like the bomb baby. Tiny, blackened, ragged, babbling softly in delirium, it's the small transvestite's burnt baby brother, the weak-armed flame dancer.

Nobody is nursing any of these wretched young people. Father Gaudi reaches into the high collar of his robe and pulls out a silver locket. He removes sacred bread and works his way around the room, slipping the sacrament into gasping mouths.

"Body of—"

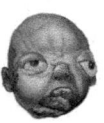

"—Christ, eh, Love?" says Imelda, in another back room. She's holding down the golden-eyed girl with one hand, and trying to gag her with the other. "This is as close as you're getting to communion for a long time."

Unbathed and untreated, the girl is barely recognizable through her cuts and contusions. "I'm sorry, Den Mother,

Bomb Baby

I'm sorry! I won't run again! It's just that the old American smelled so bad, like poisonous gas! I couldn't help it, I couldn't breathe!"

The sound of some non-sidelined Filipinas practicing a hymn comes sweetly down the corridor.

"Hear your older sisters' music? They sing for you. They've been through this, and I as well, and we survived. You will, also. It's part of the burden of being a grown-up lady. So don't spoil their song with unhappy sounds from your own throat. Bite this rag."

"But I want to pray to the Blessed Virgin for forgiveness. Please, Den Mother, may I?"

"Of course, Love. And I'll join you."

As they say the Lord's Prayer together in Tagalog, Ishida-san's reptilian lieutenant approaches very slowly from the opposite corner, his stockinged feet whistling along the quaintly traditional tatami mats. Over his head he swings a stout bamboo rod. The closer he gets, the wider the girl's eyes grow. She's going to start screaming any moment.

"There, there," murmurs Imelda. "It's not quite as much fun as running down the sidewalk in the night like a wild puppy-dog. But it's better than being back in our homeland, isn't it? Be strong now, and the old man might not have you deported."

Even while struggling to insert the rag, Imelda modestly averts her eyes. Her role model is the Virgin Mary, after all. She gazes soulfully out the window.

"Come now, bite down on this rag. It's better than chewing your tongue off. And we wouldn't want to bother the neighbors."

She can see Father Gaudi taking his leave of the Yakuza office. He pauses to make the sign of the cross on the forehead of the sentry, who still weeps.

To the lieutenant, Imelda says, "Okay, okay Godzilla, you made your point. Hurry up and get this Jezebel chastised. It's almost time for mass."

Later that afternoon, at the Hiroshima Cathedral compound, a wedding rehearsal is being conducted. The Filipinas and the transvestites are gathered around the Yakuza vans, singing their hymn. Their toddlers bounce around in the drivers' seats, twist the steering wheels and beep the horns. The thug drivers are nowhere to be seen.

A big spider has strung a web across the baby abandonment drawer. Dead black butterflies hang there. It has not been used for some time.

Bomb Baby

In the crypt chapel, Father Gaudi gingerly inserts a consecrated wafer between the enameled lips of Imelda, trying not to cringe as he says, "Body of Christ."

Chomping and burping, she replies. "Amen."

The usual foreigners, including Hank, Polly and the Japanese amateur archaeologist, are seated in their regular places. Only the auto executives' wives are absent. They have been driven away, and thugs have taken over the front pew.

These are the same guys who wore rental tuxes at the previous wedding, and reluctantly chased the bomb baby. Now they sport their customary crass mobster-style outfits and lounge around, comfortable as Christians. They seem pretty confident that the "unlucky spirit" will not be showing up today to scare them away.

A playful thug rises to his feet, sneaks up from behind, and pinches Imelda's big butt. In response, she folds her hands over her matronly bust and raises her sopping eyes to the ceiling. She is doing an excellent impression of the saccharine painting of the Blessed Virgin scotch-taped to the concrete wall. Imelda rises from the communion rail, genuflects, and turns to join the thugs in the front pew.

The mutterings of several indignant foreigners can be heard—

"Why does this greasy crone get to come in, and not the lovely young Filipinas?"

"It's the privilege of rank. She's the recruiter. She lures her little sisters out of the jungle with promises of legitimate work in the land of golden opportunity."

"Chunky broad finally shows her face."

Tom Bradley

"What's to stop her? She has all the bodyguards she needs, squatting right next to her."

A few thugs kneel at the communion rail, and refuse to scoot over for the actual Christians. They open their mouths wide and arch their backs like trained seals at a marina, expecting to be offered a slug of nice wine. But Father Gaudi just gives them the same tender forehead blessing he gives to sentries and babies.

More disgruntled mutters—

"While the cat's away..."

"Why don't they unlock their Sherman tanks and let the girls come in and be treated like human beings for forty-five minutes or so?"

"Think of the degrading acts the Filipinas must perform every night. Feeling human cuts into the quality of their work."

In the back of the crypt, some muscular young foreigners are removing their Sunday-best blazers and murmuring anti-Japanese sentiments in each others' ears. The Nigerian acolyte nudges Father Gaudi, who looks up and sees a brawl brewing. He mounts the pulpit and clears his throat, bringing the place to order. At the communion rail, the thugs turn around and sit on the purple velvet knee-cushions, facing the congregation.

"My friends," says the priest, "before our customary social hour gets underway, allow me to say one thing. I will speak over our guests' heads, as they're the only ones present who have no English. Please try to remember that these poor fellows fit no better into the mainstream than we do. So, even though they are indigenous to the re-

Bomb Baby

gion—and even though we all love to Japan-bash from time to time—let us try to tolerate their presence. Still better, let us welcome them as lovingly as we can."

"Fine," says someone, "but why isn't the Pimp-of-Pimps down here to bask in our snuggly love? Is he too good for our company Or just too busy destroying people's lives?"

The amateur archaeologist says, "No. Ishida-San's too busy destroying the past."

"What's that supposed to mean?" asks Hank.

In response, the archaeologist commences singing, "O'er the land of the freeeeee, and the..."

"Been there," says Hank.

The archaeologist says, "The warlord who founded Hiroshima four hundred years ago kept his harem on that very spot. The soil bristles with priceless, sexy relics."

"Well, *banzai* to that!" says someone. "Bastard's a real patriot."

"So, Gaudi," says Hank, "is that why the Godfather doesn't hang out with us? Because he's too busy burying Japan's proud cultural heritage under slabs of concrete?"

"Let's just say that, unlike his followers, Ishida-san instinctively knows that a non-believer shouldn't come too close to Christ's body and blood." Father Gaudi gently slaps a thug's hand away from the sacramental wine.

Polly stands, clears her throat, and says, "Speaking of blood, if anybody's still interested, I have my husband's first and, I guess, final report to the Angler's Education Committee. I've been assuming the committee was dissolved, by default, so to speak."

She looks pointedly at the thugs and Imelda, and unfolds a scribbled-upon doughnut wrapper from her pocket.

"But I might as well present Sammy's report to you now." (reading aloud) "Fish-hooks are too dangerous. The stupid little prick pokes himself."

"So," says Father Gaudi, "the subject of the bomb baby has been officially broached."

Imelda, who has absorbed every word of the discussion so far, falls to her knees in feigned prayer so she can pretend not to listen to the rest.

"You all seem to have figured it out by now," says Father Gaudi. "Our small, strange friend has finally fulfilled everybody's worst expectations, and vanished."

Someone suggests, "What about contacting the proper authorities?"

Everybody laughs at that suggestion. "Honey, you just try to get the Hiroshima fuzz interested in a transient on the slowest day of the year."

Hank shouts, "I move to reconvene the Anglers' Education Committee!" He meets little difficulty getting the motion seconded.

Polly says, "Sammy has no time to conduct a manhunt. He's a professor—"

"Exactly," sneers Hank. "He has more time than he knows what to do with. Besides, he knew the bomb baby better than anybody."

"Hear, hear!" cry various foreigners. "Man-hunt, man-hunt!"

Bomb Baby

Without comprehension, but cheerfully, the thugs join in.

To Hank, Polly says, "...*knew* the bomb baby?"

"Sorry," he smirks.

The Nigerian acolyte props the fake silk screen in front of the altar. With a sigh, the social hour gets halfheartedly rolling. The thugs remain seated on the communion rail knee cushions, silently chain smoking. They watch Imelda trying to socialize like a normal Catholic society matron.

Nobody will talk to her, or even stand near her. Like a madwoman, she gossips and titters into empty space.

Outside, Sam is snoring, as usual, in the death seat of the Mazda. As Yakuza gum wrappers sail through the open window to collect on his lolling tongue, he has a nightmare—

Like a Satanist coven, the foreigners squat in vulgar positions around the crypt altar. They yowl this cannibal hymn:

Tom Bradley

Pluck forth thy royal diadems.
Pluck forth thy locks entwined within.
Pluck forth from radiant brows the flesh
which pads the seams where head-bones mesh.

The archaeologist rummages among a treasure trove of sacred objects on the floor. He comes up shouldering a golden shovel.

Pry back thy scalp like fecund sod.
Expose thy rank farm's protein pods.
Chip free thy skull, let marrow drain,
Till one gray tegument remains.

Imelda climbs onto the altar with amorous intentions. She gropes the crucifix.

And when thy brain is amply shown,
and naught is left of skin and bone...

Father Gaudi has an insane look on his face. He wields a crude ceramic chalice.

...then serve thyself to Christus Rex...

It sloshes with gobs of human gore.

...or suffer our collective hex.

Bomb Baby

The Mazda convulses on its worn-out shocks as Sam lurches awake from this horrible vision. He sticks his face out the window, gasping for air, his whole body throbbing with panicked heartbeat.

Now we know why he sleeps in the car on Sunday instead of joining his wife in the crypt.

VI.

Deep into the Hiroshima night, at the riverside construction site, work is being done around the clock, to realize Ishida-san's dream as quickly as possible. Covering the fresh facade of his new gambling den is a bright array of neon lights, which reads—

HOME OF THE BRAVE

In the shadows at the periphery, the archaeologist turns over a few shovelfuls of mud, and does indeed discover a piece of ancient pottery.

No longer caring if he is seen trespassing, he pockets his find and treks out across the construction area, toward a large house trailer. On its front awning is hung the sinister looking emblem of Ishida-san's underworld organization, big and conspicuous in the artificial light.

The lieutenant sits on the front stoop, chatting with a couple of teen biker punks. They wear purple and green spike hairdos, brown lipstick, and buttock-exposing cutaway leather jeans. On the backs of their jackets is emblazoned the name of their motorcycle gang:

Bomb Baby

THE KELOID KROWD

When the archaeologist comes striding suddenly out of the night, the lieutenant knocks him flat on his back and removes the contents of his pockets. He passes the ancient artifact through the trailer window to Ishida-san, who has pulled back the curtain in mild curiosity.

The archaeologist's voice can be heard, muffled under the Lieutenant's shoe. "Bribe me generously, or I go public with that pot shard and all work ceases around here!"

Ishida-san nods his head gently at the lieutenant, and retires from the window. The razor-sharp blade of an exquisitely-crafted Samurai knife glints in the artificial light.

"See now," says the lieutenant to the two punks, "you don't just jab straight on like this. His sternum gets in the way."

When the tip of the knife clicks against the archaeologist's breast bone, he looks more surprised than pained.

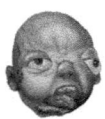

The house trailer has a lavishly appointed interior, complete with black-velvet paintings of golden-eyed tigers, a bar, and even a fake European-style fireplace with a deep mantelpiece.

As the lecture-demonstration continues outside, Ishida-san settles himself comfortably in a green leather arm-

73

chair. He examines the pot shard and listens to what's happening outside.

"This is the angle, between these two ribs. Slice in, pretty hard, to get through those muscle fibers, and then up... You don't have to be so polite about it! I mean really up! Try again...Okay now, watch his eyes. Count to ten..."

Ishida-san stands, crosses his office, and arranges his new curio attractively on his ersatz mantelpiece. He steps back, squints his eyes, and tilts his head to check the effect in this particular angle of light.

The lieutenant is saying, "See that? The life goes out at a relaxed pace, and he sort of snuggles into himself with a sigh, like a tired baby at bedtime. That's because you just sliced his left ventricle in two, in the efficient and effective manner of our proud Samurai ancestors."

The first punk observes, "With his eyes bugged out like that, and that beard, he looks just like a foreigner."

"It's best not to look at their eyes too much after you've tucked them in," says the lieutenant. "Their soul is looking for a place to hide from the devil, and it might just choose your body... And now, you ignorant punks, I want you to think hard. Under these circumstances, do I even need to ask how we dispose of our handiwork?"

Ishida-san hears this last question, breaks into a small, fond smile, and gazes across the site of his future dream palace, at the roaring cement mixer.

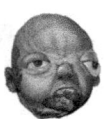

Bomb Baby

In the upstream suburbs around noon, Sam Edwine is standing in the stern of a noisy speedboat. At the wheel is a teenaged Japanese boatman. He sports an oily pompadour that droops over his face.

They speed up and down the rich neighborhoods. Sam lurches from rail to rail, almost capsizing the boat. He is trying to make this manhunt as conspicuous as possible. Even on this chaotic river, Sam manages to create a nuisance. He nearly capsizes several small fishing boats with his wake.

"Yoo-hoo, Mr. Bomb Bay-Be-e-e-e! Where on earth can the naughty boy be?"

He waves and screams at the American auto executives' baby sitters. These native girls are taking white toddlers for a stroll along the bank. They are average examples of their kind. But, to the local way of seeing, their blue eyes and blond hair epitomize everything perfect and lovely. Every fisherman on the water and every pedestrian on the land stares at the toddlers in adoration.

Sam shrieks at the baby sitters. "Young ladies, do you see me? I am searching high and low for your mistress' muddy mouser! Now will you ask them to get out of my wife's face, please?"

The toddlers laugh at him, but Sam gets no other reaction whatever. The baby sitters barely raise their eyes. They are modest Japanese virgins of good social class, after all—which makes it all the more surprising when they abandon the toddlers and duck into a nearby bamboo grove.

Tom Bradley

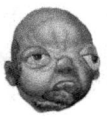

A dope-peddling bum has parked his rickety bicycle in this grove. He's one of the sweet old guys who stood on tiptoe and stroked Sam's beard at the A-bomb Golden Jubilee celebration. But he's been corrupted in the meantime.

With hunger in their eyes, the baby sitters converge on him and purchase little bags of yellow crystalline powder—Mamoon's sinister concoction.

At the American auto company's R&D facility, Sam orders his teenaged boatman to make several especially obnoxious runs under the balcony of Hank's laboratory.

Hank is standing by the back door, whittling on a futuristic model car, a white lab coat protecting his spiffy brushed denims. His lab seems to be a buzzing hive of automotive creativity.

Through the windows, about a half-dozen Japanese lab assistants can be seen scurrying and scrambling among vats of high-tech inorganic sculpting plasticine, extra-large computer display terminals and gyroscope-mounted drawing boards.

Bomb Baby

"Hank! Hankie-e-e!" screams Sam. "Have you seen the bomb baby, you prick?" To the boatman, he says, "Is that all the louder you can rev this bathtub toy?"

He kicks and dents the chrome exhaust manifold, hoping to jar the already ineffective muffler loose. But, when Hank comes strolling out onto the pier, Sam cries, "I changed my mind! Whoa! Steady, big fella! Holding pattern! Stop, for Christ's sake!"

The boatman puts it in idle.

"Edwine? What are you doing up here in the suburbs? You're supposed to be cruising the docks. That's where a bunch of the other homeless types hang out. The bomb baby's probably on a bender with his colleagues."

Sam screams, to be heard over the outboards. "This teeny-bopper says we can't go to the docks! It's against Ministry of Tourism regulations! The city fathers will lose face if an important foreigner like me sees that the third world is alive and well, right here in Hiroshima!"

"Lies."

"Beg-pardon?"

Sam nudges his giant knee into the boatman's spinal column. This persuades him to cut the engines altogether. He tosses a line to Hank, who makes no effort to catch it.

Hank seats himself on the pier. "I said, your sidekick is just lying through his teeth. You can take that boat wherever the water's deep enough to buoy the props out of the mud. That's the whole point, Edwine. The Angler's Education Committee appointed you to find the bomb baby before the city fathers start regulating river traffic."

"Whatever. Why don't you invite me into your lab for a nice cup of tea or Jack Daniels or something? I'm a fellow American. Where's your hospi-goddamn-tality?"

"Top secret things in there. All the dope on next year's models. You could be an industrial spy."

"So I'll give you beers. We've got an on-board ice chest. Join us in our manhunt, and we'll scour the soggy slums together. Being all alone on a boat with someone like this is creepy."

"I'm afraid I just can't up and desert. I work for industry. I'm involved in the research and development of useful things. Unlike you academic slobs, I have to punch in a certain number of hours each day. So I'll have to take a rain check on your invi—"

Suddenly, the sound of loud martial music from the opposite bank cuts Hank off in mid-sentence. It's the male college cheerleaders whom we saw earlier at the A-Bomb Golden Anniversary Celebration. They are marching by, on maneuvers. The thinner underclass underlings are being forced to trudge barefoot in the mud of the flood plain.

Sam's nervous student straggles among them. He has neither the physical strength nor the emotional energy for this. The boy looks ready to collapse any minute. He pops a handful of his pharmaceutical uppers.

Sam laughs. "Smile and wave at the noodle-Nazis, Hankums!"

Hank is appalled. "Who are those horrible boys?"

"My campus is infested with them. As a matter of fact, I think I see one of my freshmen over there... Yoo-hoo, Freshboy-san! Have you done your homework?"

Bomb Baby

"Don't do that! They'll see us!"

The nervous student pretends not to notice Sam, and tries to disappear into the marching ranks. The Cheerleaders approach a point directly across the Ohtagawa. To the accompaniment of a mammoth bass drum, they start to scream fascist songs from the thirties and forties.

Hank gets even more panicky. Something about these boys and their music terrorizes him to the depths of his cardiovascular system. He throws himself flat on his belly on the pier and mutters, "I can't hear myself breathe!"

"Well, Hankie, if you're sure you don't want to join us, I guess we'll be shoving off. Bye now. Take care of yourself."

"You're not leaving me here!"

Hank leaps into the boat. A true professional, even in his panic, he is able to shout a few Japanese words of highly technical instruction to his native lab assistants, who have meanwhile gathered at the back door.

"Okay!" Sam tells the boatman. "Chart a course for the funkier distributaries!"

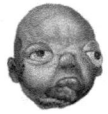

They head downstream, weaving and veering in and out of the unregulated traffic, like a damp bumper-car ride. After the horizon has swallowed up the cheerleaders, Sam pops a couple beers from the on-board ice chest. Hank gradually regains composure.

Tom Bradley

The boat passes within sight of Hiroshima University, Sam's place of employment. A mysterious shoe box-like structure occupies a brown knoll at the edge of the campus. It's the med school's mental health clinic.

Hank says, "Boom Town U.'s loony bin. You know, of course, Professor, that eventually you're going to have to look in there."

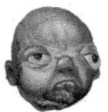

At the docks are the campsites of Hiroshima's outcasts. Tucked into every nook and cranny, they're jealously guarding vast, pointless accumulations of junk-wealth: washing-machine cartons bursting with bottle caps and bales of meticulously origamied ice cream wrappers.

Here, too, as in Peace Park, we see some bums of the bomb baby's exact age, who got A-bombed inside their mother's bellies and are deformed or mentally retarded.

Hank says, "I don't know about the women—what few specimens there are—but if the men are away from their families for more than seven months, they're declared legally dead. Juvenile delinquents are free to stomp them to mush and set them on fire, without fear of legal entanglement. And the old folks right here are in particular danger, living as they do on the border of—"

The speedboat snuggles beneath a highway overpass.

"—Biker Land!"

Bomb Baby

On the bank, the Keloid Krowd, in outlandish punk-derivative garb, are working on their motorcycles and hot rods. These evil adolescent bikers have covered every surface with beautiful graffiti. Skulls and mushroom clouds are spray-painted everywhere with effortless clarity.

The Keloid Krowd clubhouse is a lean-to built from scrap materials. Inside, with a couple of rusty aluminum rat-tail combs, the two punks are practicing the lieutenant's ventricle-stabbing techniques on an aged wino. So far, they've only succeeded in injuring him.

When they hear the sounds of the speedboat, they abandon their practice and run outside.

The punks join their comrades in manning the throttles of their various vehicles. The Keloid Krowd revs in unison, trying to run the speedboat off with a blast of infernal racket from unmuffled engines.

Hank shouts, "I'm told the great Ishida-san recruits his assassins here."

"What, these weenies on their whiny rice burners? Not in a zillion years. Let's go dig up some more honest, burping bums. Gun it!"

Nothing happens. The boatman is paralyzed with biker-horror. It's necessary to pry his fingers from the steering wheel so Hank can get the boat moving again.

By the time they've gotten a bit further downstream, the boatman has recovered the use of his body, and he's been ordered to cruise under grimy turnpike bridges.

Behind chain-link fences, on the graveled edges of destitute embankments, the homesteads of hoboes can be seen. Sam orders the outboards to be put in neutral, and they drift awhile. The river has almost no current here.

Hank says, "Guess what's the leading cause of death among these homeless Japanese. I'll give you a hint. It's not exposure to the elements, and it's not—" (pausing significantly) "*dangerous drugs.*"

"Don't tell me about it. Not a word. I don't want to hear about the schemes you and Mamoon have got cooking."

The idling boat runs aground at the edge of a particularly strange campsite. This space has been staked out by a man with thick aviator glasses and a nylon training jacket emblazoned with these words—

Bomb Baby

BEEF-MASTER

In his shaded spread he possesses two separate herds of one-eyed alley cats, and meters of random weeds strung up and curing over miniature styrofoam bonfires. The boat sits motionless, while Sam and this cat rancher share what feels like a five minute stare-down.

Sam says, "Do you think our Huckleberry friend hopped a freight barge for the balmy coral beaches of Okinawa?"

The cat rancher makes no reply, but gathers an armload of cats to his breast. Only his tears betray him.

"He's mourning for someone," says Hank.

"You miss B.B., don't you?" Sam asks him. Then he addresses the neighboring hoboes. "You all miss him, right?"

While Sam sermonizes the huddled masses, Hank leans over the speedboat rail and peers deep into the nooks and crannies of the embankment. He clears his throat loudly, as if cuing someone to come out of hiding. And, sure enough, Mamoon creeps from behind a pile of discarded futons, toting his little black bag full of blood-collecting paraphernalia.

Not noticing the Bangladeshi radiation researcher, Sam says, "These folks need the bomb baby as badly as Calcuttans need Mother Teresa. This is his home and his ministry. Somebody has to bring him back soon."

Finally seeing Mamoon, Sam grins and yells, "What a surprise! It's almost as though you had an appointment to meet us here! How's the Bruiser treating you? Any new welts under those little britches?"

"As I've told you many times before, Dr. Edwine, my supervisor's name happens to be Valentina. And she never touches me." He squats down and ties off the cat rancher's biceps.

"Don't be coy," chuckles Sam. "I know the pair of you are whipping up a race of tiny Paki-Russky hybrids to continue your work for the next 200 years."

"Make that *Bangladeshi*-Russky hybrids," says Hank.

To the cat rancher, Mamoon says, "Make a fist, if you would be so kind... So, who—rather, what brings you all the way down here, Dr. Edwine?"

"God sent me to look for your main source of plasma. I didn't know you had so many backups, or I wouldn't have bothered."

"Yes, these tidewater transients are fascinating subjects for liver biopsies as well. Very promising. I can almost taste the mutations." Mamoon wrestles with the cat rancher, who's not fond of needles. "And they're much easier to handle than the bomb baby... Have you found him yet?"

"Do you think I'd be floating around with this pony-tailed dip-wad if I knew where Hiroshima's real good-time boy was?"

"I suppose not." Mamoon pokes around inside the cat rancher for an artery. "Did you know that the main cause of death among these unfortunate people is not the ingestion of—"

"Dangerous drugs," leers Hank. "The professor knows, he knows."

Bomb Baby

Sam reaches into the on-board ice chest, grabs a sandwich, and tosses it to Mamoon, who catches it with bloody fingers, then drops it. Two or three bums appear, snatch it up, and vanish back into the shadows, fighting over the gory thing.

Sam settles down comfortably on the deck with a couple beers for himself—the last two. He leans over the boat rail, dangling a few languid fingers in the filthy water, and says, "Speaking of the good-time boy, the strangest rumors have been circulating among the med students at my university's nut-house. They say the bomb baby was having an affair with an actual woman before his disappearance, a lady Russky who hangs out on top of a certain creepy-crawly mountain near here..."

The smog parts briefly in the distance, revealing the Radiation Research Foundation on top of Mount Hijiyama.

"Does that ring a bell or what, Mamoon, my man?"

"I'm sure the native interns would have no difficulty imagining Valentina alone with him. They are two of a kind, at least from the Japanese point of view: just a couple of irradiated aliens. Her own genetic material was scrambled during two helicopter rides over Chernobyl.

The teen boatman is getting restless. He keeps looking back fearfully toward Biker Land. Besides being afraid of the bikers, he has never been so humiliated in all his life: here he is wasting an afternoon among homeless people and weird foreigners. He shudders and fidgets so much that the boat works itself free from the mud.

Just as Mamoon removes the needle from the cat rancher's forearm and stows the blood sample in his black bag, the boat begins to drift. The conversation continues as the boat slides very slowly down the embankment. Mamoon strolls alongside, occasionally tripping on a bum or a pile of trash, stopping only when he comes upon a wretch too weak, drunk, or catatonic to resist being vampirized.

To Hank, Sam says, "Look at your partner in crime, busily working his way from one wretch to the next. He looks just like Father Gaudi doing the drive-in ministry. Except Gaudi hands out God's flesh instead of stealing the blood of the damned."

Hank is eager to get back to the point. "The word around the automotive community is that Valentina's interested less in the bomb baby's chromosomes than his white blood cells. She's supposedly been pumping him full of HIV and sucking whole quarts of serum from his veins in the name of AIDS research."

"Oooh! Gracious sakes, no! Bite your tongue, Hankums!"

"Who are you to pooh-pooh these rumors without checking the woman out first?"

"Wait a sec... You want me to check her out?"

The boat gets stuck in a mini-doldrum. Mamoon takes advantage of the pause to squat down and drain a snickering old bag lady. He unwraps a syringe.

"Is this an order?" asks Sam. "In the sense that my wife won't be able to pray in peace unless I obey?"

"It's a firm suggestion," says Hank. "Straight from the mouth of the Chairman of the Angler's Education Committee."

Bomb Baby

Mamoon chimes in. "Valentina has a locked lab all to herself at the Foundation. She calls it her personal space. If you're serious about unearthing the poor pinhead, it might be worthwhile to insinuate yourself."

"Why don't you?" says Sam. "You spend each working day right under her nose."

Mamoon slaps the old bag lady's hand away from his crotch. "That's exactly why it would be hopeless for me to try. She is, I fear, a racist. She treats me as though I'm infected with something even worse than AIDS."

"Like, for example, halitosis? Come on now! Deliberate HIV injections? The Foundation wouldn't allow their facilities to be used for such ghoulish procedures...would they?"

Mamoon does not reply, but averts his eyes and pokes the bag lady hard to make her squeal, as a diversion. This does not reassure Sam at all. He stands up and paces the deck a bit nervously, rocking the boat out of its doldrum and making it drift again. To keep up with the Americans, Mamoon has to abandon the bag lady, the needle still in her arm.

Sam is trying to convince himself. "Besides, her results could be skewed by the bomb baby's relationships with all those lovey-dovey Christians at the cathedral. The Bruiser could never be certain that he hadn't already been infected."

As he follows alongside the boat, tiptoeing among human refuse, Mamoon exchanges glances again with Hank. The two of them begin closing in on Sam like hyenas stalking a wounded giraffe.

"I guess you're right, Edwine."

"He might very well be infected at prayer," says Mamoon. The boat drifts a little faster, and he trots to keep up.

"But not at play," says Hank.

"For example," says Mamoon, "dirty needles wouldn't be a consideration."

"B.B.'s not involved with dangerous drugs," says Hank.

Mamoon's beginning to get out of breath. "At least not from a consumeristic standpoint." He reaches across the thread of river that separates him from the speedboat, and tosses several small plastic bags of his designer dope on the deck. To Hank, he says, "By the way, here are samples of the new batch. And, if I do say so myself, it turned out quite nicely."

Hank grins. "So, Professor, the ice is broken, yeah?"

"What," says Sam, "you think I'm surprised?"

The boatman helps himself to a bag and turns his back to self-administer the drug. Sam looks away.

Hank says, "Why do you think the kid was willing to float us down here to hell? Call it a tip."

"Are you guys aware of the insane dope laws in this country?" cries Sam. "Half a joint on your bathroom floor is the same as a yacht full of heroin. In prison they let you do nothing but sit on the edge of your cot all day. Not even any fun buggery."

Hank and Mamoon leer at each other.

"You guys just keep hinting around. I'm no capitalist, and I have no interest in your enterprise. I'd much rather

Bomb Baby

talk about the chief neck-biter on top of Mount Hijiyama. Do you really think she dorked Double B.?"

Hank pulls up a deck chair and winds up for some serious coaching. He reaches into his pocket and takes out a snapshot of Valentina. She's lugging a plastic bag of cheap plum wine out of a downtown Hiroshima Seven-Eleven store.

Sam is disappointed. "Oh, never mind. Fuck this. Not my type."

Hank has a suggestion: "You could invite yourself to the Foundation and pretend to interview her for a non-existent weekly back home. Russkies still consider themselves exotic in the free world.

"I'd make a lousy spy. I've got no idea how to ask leading questions and be subtle."

"So fake it."

"Such enthusiasm, Hankster. It's almost as though you've got your own secret reasons for wanting me pawed by that commie broad."

The boat bumps gently into an abandoned trash barge and stops. The bag lady is waddling after Mamoon with a sexy look on her face. She giggles and fingers the hypo that still dangles from her arm. "You're a little lover-man, is what you are," she murmurs to the Bangladeshi.

The boatman, high now, switches on the on-board boom-box. He accidentally turns to a station that features the martial music and fascist songs which the male college cheerleaders play and scream.

Hank hears this racket, and thinks the horrible boys he fears so much have suddenly marched into the neighborhood. He clings to the rail and nearly has a stroke. Sam kicks the boom box into the water, where it bubbles and sputters awhile before sinking. The noise is drowned out by real-life screams coming from further down the embankment. To Hank's immeasurable relief, it's not the cheerleaders coming, but another sort of teenager altogether.

A pack of bikers, including the two punks, are working their way up the riverbank. They are marauding into the hoboes' campsites, stomping on everybody and threatening to set them on fire with blowtorches contrived from spray paint cans and cigarette lighters. The bikers are being egged on and cheered by the working-class grown-ups who earlier threw money into the river for the bomb baby to fetch.

Mamoon is horrified. With the bag lady hanging amorously off him, he tries to scramble on board, dropping his little black bag. The vials inside shatter. Blood splashes out and stains the embankment.

The boatman is just as scared as Mamoon. He guns the engine before the Bangladeshi can get in. Sam and Hank barely avoid being bounced overboard. Mamoon leaps for it and winds up flat on his face in the mud, choking on a black cloud of outboard exhaust, the bag lady cackling and rolling on top of him.

The boat takes off. Mamoon is left behind, screaming to be rescued. Hank is laughing so hard he nearly gags.

Bomb Baby

At the riverside construction site, as usual, Ishida-san is personally overseeing the work on his new gambling parlor. A van backs into the construction site and pulls up behind him.

A thug driver sticks his head out the window. "Um, Boss? We got one on the way out."

Ishida-san continues watching the workmen. After a while he turns and nods to his lieutenant, who deals with the problem.

Peering into the back of the van, the lieutenant asks, "Which one is it this time?"

"What, you don't recognize him? A little too well-done on that side, I guess."

The lieutenant is not prepared to exchange banter with a mere driver.

"It's the littlest cross-dresser's baby brother."

"The littlest cross-dresser?"

"Yeah, you know. The one that's always pouting and whining and crying."

"They all do that. Even the big ones."

In the back of the van, the flame dancer is thrashing and babbling. He looks and sounds a lot like the bomb baby.

"This dumb spastic dumped a whole tray of flaming benzine goblets all over himself. He's a tough little guy, though. It happened about a week ago, and he's been hanging on all this time. Looks like it's finally catching up with him now. He keeps begging to be wiped with a special magic spirit oil or something. He says it can only be found at the foreigners' shrine."

"Oh, that," says the lieutenant. "Wait a minute." He reports back to the boss.

"How was his work?" asks Ishida-san.

"Fine. While he lasted, he was a pleasure to work with, unlike his bitchy brother."

"All right. The old priest has enough sense not to make waves. Let the boy go see him. But get back here before dark—"

The archaeologist's corpse can be seen, wrapped in plastic and stuffed behind the cement mixer.

"—because you've got a little disposal job to do."

The lieutenant bows ninety degrees and returns to the van. He gets in the death seat and is about to close the door, when he hears his master's voice—

"Tell Father I said hello! And give him my best!"

VII.

It's dusk at the Radiation Research Foundation. A Hiroshima city bus pulls into the acid rain-ravaged bamboo
grove at the summit of Mount Hijiyama. Sam disembarks
with dozens of aging A-bomb victims.

Among them are several of the bums from Peace Park,
Sam's pals. He's exchanging caresses with them and trying
to buck up their courage to face the horrors of this place.
One by one, everybody but Sam heads for various flapping
doors marked—

LIVER BIOPSIES
BLOOD SCREENINGS
FOETAL TISSUE SAMPLES
STOOLS
URINE

The bums are enticed by orderlies with trays of cold
rice balls and cans of cheap chemical beer.

Sam wanders out back and approaches a Quonset hut
marked with a sign that reads:

RADIATION EFFECTS CAFETERIA

Tom Bradley

To reach this goal, he picks his way through a medical wasteland: a forest of mops planted in buckets, sheaves of exposed X-ray film and discarded syringes.

Inside, he shudders when Ray Conniff's rendition of "Red Roses for a Blue Lady" hisses down the back of his neck. He scans the rows of pastel aluminum tables and easily picks out Valentina from among the dozens of international radiation researchers. She's the one waving a bottle of cut-rate plum wine in his direction.

On her table are two ice-filled Mason jars and two bowls of macaroni and cheese. The chairs are the form-fitting fiberglass kind found usually in bowling alleys. Valentina starts eating with one hand. With the other she pulls snapshots of grandchildren from a handbag and deals them like cards across the table.

"A budding anarchist, that one," she grunts. "But very clever... The words *amoebic dysentery* seem not to be in his physiological vocabulary."

"Huh? Whose—?"

"You know who I am talking about. Your pin-headed bomb baby virtually subsists on raw sewage. If you're looking for some evidence of mutation, tag a few of his leukocytes and trail them like rafts through his bloodstream."

"There'll be no tagging anything on the bomb baby. He's vanished. I thought you'd heard. It's all over the, um, Christian community, and—"

"Anyway, it does not matter. We two are all that matters. Correct? Look at us—" She grabs Sam's arm and pushes his tweed sleeve up to his elbow. She holds out her own equally pale forearm for comparison. "See? Identical shades. We are the same. *Onaji-da,* as the locals so primitively put it. Even our leaders are clones. Ignorant clones both of them. Handsome performers with red ball noses, like in the circus. Just clones."

"Clowns or clones?"

"Exactly!"

Sam is at a loss for words. Since this woman is obviously drunk already, he swigs down his wine and pours more.

"Yes," says Valentina, grandly, "now is indeed a time for clones. You and I, Samsha, we can be big blue-eyed clones, too. We must mount a performance. We have a responsibility to let the readers of your hometown weekly gazette know that the cold war is really over, so they can get back to their births, defecations and deaths in a peaceful frame of mind."

She reaches across the table and grabs him by the tweed lapels. "And we must notify our Nipponese hosts that they are now redundant. A Pacific buffer between our two great Caucasoid civilizations is no longer necessary."

She waves her arm at the surrounding tables. "These island dwarves are on their way down. Their pitiful spit-bubble has burst. Soon you and I will be riding rickshaws to work, Samsha, and paying the fare with half-smoked cigarette stubs. The natives will dive and scramble to suck the simple carbohydrates from our discarded chewing gum wrappers..."

She hammers back her fourth jar with grace worthy of a Bolshoi ballerina. "This is not Ukrainian *spiritus* in our glasses. Far from it. But, no matter. Friendship is the only intoxicant we need. Together let us now sing the *Internationale*."

"Um... I never really learned that one."

"So we will sing something else in duple time. Tell me you're not too immature to have heard of Pyotr Seeger. And his smash hit..."

They stand up, toast each other, link arms, and sing:

May there always be sunshine!
May there always be blue skies!
May there always be Mommy!
May there always be me!

Valentina belches. "Drink to the first of two centuries on this squalid mountain!"

They remain coupled, their bodies swaying with alcohol.

"Now, my Samsha, come, let us visit my personal space. I will show you secret things. One of my so-called patients is waiting just for you!"

They lumber to their feet and she leads him drunkenly through the labyrinthine and creepy bowels of the foundation. In Valentina's lab, the aging radiation victim still hovers over his strapped-down retarded sister. The pair of them have been languishing here ever since the A-bomb Golden Jubilee.

"Let us dispose of these miserable creatures. And then—ah!—we have so many things to discuss! For example, the amusing pharmaceutical project on which our

Bomb Baby

funny friend from Bangladesh has been working so hard, like a naughty elf... Samsha, as a professor with daily access to classrooms full of, shall we say, *potential customers...*"

Sam shudders at those words. Without wanting to, he suddenly gets a mental picture of himself at his working environment—

In his classroom at Hiroshima U., he has his feet up on the teacher's desk, a coke and a doughnut balanced on his belly, and he's dozing off. Most of his freshmen are asleep, too.

He hears Valentina saying, "You might be interested in the commercial applications..."

Everybody looks as though they could use a central nervous system stimulant, except the male college cheerleaders. These junior fascists sit ramrod straight, in full uniform. They seem very angry about their tuition money being used to pay this decadent American to sleep. Some of them look ready to rise up and awaken him in violent ways. The only thing holding them back is Sam's ominous size, especially juxtaposed with the tiny East Asian teacher's desk. It would be safer to poke a hibernating grizzly bear with a stick.

Valentina is saying, "My little brown research assistant already has the high schools, how do you say, covered. He is ready to graduate to higher learning, Professor Sam-sha..."

Sam's nervous student twitches among the cheerleaders. He can't stand the tension. He reaches into his pocket and takes out his little bottle of pharmaceutical pills.

"Of course," says Valentina, "as a citizen of the former Soviet Union, I am ignorant as a baby about concepts like supply and demand..."

To the boy's horror, no pills are left.

"But Mamoon assures me there's plenty of the latter at your place of employment..."

The nervous student scampers out of the classroom in panic, almost awakening Sam. Out the window, he can be seen scrambling across the campus to the mental health clinic on its brown knoll. The place is closed. He waves his empty prescription bottle around and kicks frantically at the doors.

Sam snores once and wakes himself up, just in time to spill the coke all over his belly.

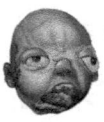

In her lab, Valentina is saying, "I presume that's really why you have come to me, the vanished river tramp notwithstanding, and all coyness aside, eh?"

The aging radiation victim's retarded sister suddenly lets out a wail, causing Sam to jump. Squares of red-splotched gauze are draped and patched across her face

Bomb Baby

and neck. She is obviously the victim of out-of-control tissue harvesting. Her eyes are full of animal fear.

"Back to work. Come, Samsha! You can assist..."

The Bruiser places her hand on his shoulder, and Sam scrambles for the exit. He stumbles through the maze of lightless corridors, trying to retrace his steps. He passes many laboratories and sees white-coated researchers of every nationality and race performing ghoulish procedures on radiation victims. Through drunken eyes, he thinks he sees the bag lady being vivisected in a broom closet.

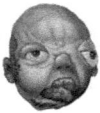

Outside, it's deep night time. He peers over the mountain's edge, looking for an escape route, then drunkenly lumbers down the slope and makes his way toward nuked downtown.

Sam enters the Hiroshima Cathedral compound by the side gate, just in time for evening mass. He stands in the shadows for a while, observing Father Gaudi.

Tom Bradley

Yakuza vans slowly pull up and arrange themselves in somber rows. Father Gaudi weaves in and out among them, dressed in his full-length black cassock, performing his drive-in ministry. The cannibal hymn seems to filter up from the crypt—

Pry back thy scalp like fecund sod...

Sam starts to run away, but Father Gaudi is beckoning him. Obediently, he trails the priest through the automotive maze, watching him slip the holy communion through van windows to sleepy Filipinas, and bless their slumbering babies.

Father Gaudi says, "I never understood why they hated him so much."   (to the pretty Filipina) "The body of Christ."

"Amen."

"Why who hated him so much?" asks Sam.

"Did they fear his bringing ritual taint into their weddings?" (to the small transvestite) "The body of Christ."

"Amen... Father! You must look in that van over there!"

The priest doesn't hear that. "Why do you never join us in the crypt, Dr. Edwine?"

Sam is startled by the abrupt change of subject. "Do you really want to know?"

More echoes of the cannibal hymn—

Chip free thy skull, let marrow drain...

Bomb Baby

"Because the child inside me is sure I'll find gore in your holy cup."

Father Gaudi winces. He looks away from Sam and into the rear of a van. Then he winces again, twice as hard.

"I think it is time for you to report back to the Angler's Education Committee, Dr. Edwine."

At first sight, it looks as though the bomb baby is lying back there. But it's actually the flame dancer, burnt, ragged and blackened. He nuzzles at the stem of a small pewter opium pipe.

"The body of Christ."

Very weakly, the flame dancer replies, "Amen...They are kind men... They give me the pipe to soothe my burns... Please don't be angry with them, Father... Please don't ban them from mass... or Den Mother..." He shudders at the mention of that vindictive demoness, then passes out.

Father Gaudi whispers, "I dare not call an ambulance. The police will get involved, and Immigration too. Ishida-san will tell them to deport all the young people from his village. His family will be blamed and the jungle will swallow them up. This child will never see his parents again."

Father Gaudi grabs Sam's elbow and pulls him out of the earshot of the thug driver, who sits in the driver's seat, fidgeting the rearview mirror up and down, checking out Sam's ominous dimensions in reverse.

"We must get him to a private hospital. We need somebody discreet with a car. I'm sure that chauffeur is well armed. But, alone, the Yakuza are unbelievable cowards. On the other hand, his cronies may come out of the chapel at any minute. Where is your car?"

Sam shrugs.

"Whom do we know with a car?"

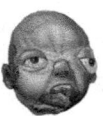

Hank's car unsteadily worms among the night traffic. It's disguised as a standard off-white Japanese sub-compact, but under the hood is an experimental electric motor. The car is silent but for the swish of smog against its front bumper, and the light suction sounds of its tire treads kissing the asphalt.

Sam is wedged into the death seat. Hank's at the wheel, having been summoned from a party. Obviously high on some sort of stimulant, he's doing a Beaver Cleaver imitation.

"Gee whillikers, Mom. How long before we're almost there yet?"

In the back seat, the flame dancer is propped and, to all appearances, dying.

"What," chuckles Hank, "no pithy last words? Lawrence the fricasseed martyr said, 'I'm done on this side. You can turn me over now.'"

Sam stares at his fellow American. "Phoning you seemed like a good idea, at the time. To Gaudi and me both."

Bomb Baby

"You dorks were sure eager to dump your difficulties in someone else's lap."

"Turn here."

Hank goes straight.

"The burn-and-trauma clinic is that way—oh. You're going to—"

"Boom Town U.'s loony bin. You got it on the first guess, Professor." Hank laughs. "It's the only alternative. You're one of their sensei: old Doc Edwine, right? So the clinic can't turn this kid away. Do you think any other medics in town would even glance at a mere penniless Flip?"

Sam looks in the back seat. In a random flash from the streetlights, he hallucinates the bomb baby lying there instead of the flame dancer.

"Besides," says Hank, "you're still the Official Emissary of the Angler's Education Committee, and I'm the Chairman..."

Sam could swear he sees the bomb baby, leering, winking, waving the flame dancer's opium pipe around, and making dopey faces.

Hank says, "We can snoop around in the varsity whacky-shack, and kill two crows with one stone, if you know what I mean." As though it's not obvious what he means, he twists his face into a grimace resembling the bomb baby's.

"But this person's not crazy."

"This person, as you call him, this craven little bugger-stuffer, is on his way out. He's way past the survivable percentage of flambéed body area."

"That's your diagnosis?"

"You betcha—as they say in one's hometown. So it doesn't matter where we go. We're just doing this to keep Father Gaudi peaceful as possible inside. We Americans owe the old guy that much, after nuking him fifty years ago."

On the way to Hiroshima University, Hank's electric car silently prowls through the same elegant lanes that Mamoon visited with Imelda. It's the wealthy residential neighborhood.

"Can you feel it?" asks Hank.

"I'm a solid bourgeois professor, and a husband."

"So what? You can feel it, right?"

"It's the duty of a man like me to look blankly across the seat at a man like you, and say... Can I feel what?"

"Don't bullshit. We're Americans. Each of us knows exactly what's on the other's mind right now. No further word needs to be spoken. Just rolling blindly through this place, guys with our demographics can feel it."

The car is driving past many heartlessly affluent homes, cold and dead as gemstones.

"All right," sighs Sam. "Fine. I'll say what you want to hear. Somebody with access to the adolescents of this neighborhood couldn't avoid making a fortune."

Bomb Baby

Hank laughs again. "Did you hear how snooty your voice got when you said *adolescents*? You college professors really do consider yourselves a cut above us mere toilers in the teen trenches."

The car passes some high school students slouching along the sidewalk. Even though it's pretty late at night, they wear uniforms and carry satchels full of books. They're trudging home from compulsory after-hours cram school, looking exhausted, bored, hopeless and bitter. Several of them crossed Sam's path at the A-Bomb Jubilee celebration. They are noticeably thinner and sicker now, due to substance abuse.

Hank is saying, "The kids are forced to lead such regimented lives. We couldn't find a single teeny-bopper with a free minute to work for us. And, with my white face and Mamoon's brown face, there's no way we could get involved on the retail end. Guys like us stand out like African-Americans at a ski resort."

Hank expects Sam to chuckle at this bit of racism, but he doesn't.

"Why are you burdening me with this?"

Hank ignores the question. "So we thought we'd try resurrecting the old myth of the dirty degenerate pusherman drooling in the suburban shadows..."

The dope-peddling bum who served the baby sitters' needs can be seen parking his rickety bicycle behind a bush.

"For the sales force, we hire only rootless transients. The homeless don't officially exist in Japan, so nobody sees them. They're especially invisible in swanky neighborhoods like this. Rich Japanese eyes flinch from shabbiness like it was leprosy... And that's where the really big pain in the butt begins. We go through about one-point-eight distribution people per month."

"What do you mean, *go through*?"

The flame dancer starts to moan and babble deliriously in his native Tagalog. Hank is unmoved by these sounds of pain and anguish coming from his back seat. He pulls up to the curb and parks, the better to take his time answering Sam's question.

"I mean they disappear. Nobody seems to know what becomes of them. The law never catches them, that's for sure. If our people get arrested, they just fill out the standard apology forms for vagrancy and loitering, and that's as hot as it ever gets. It's not even necessary to pay anybody off. Only the flatfeet from the sub-station get involved, never prefectural police. And the flatfeet wouldn't know paraphernalia if it was jabbed in their jugular. They've been in Ishida-san's pocket for so long, they've forgotten what society's enemies look like. Especially freelancers like us." (glancing back at the Flame Dancer) "It's really a privilege to live and do business in such a law-abiding society as this, don't you think?"

"To hell with you, and Mamoon, both at once." Sam reaches his huge hand over the stick shift, grabs Hank by the spiffy brushed-denim collar, and offers to throttle him. "Enough. Take this child to a doctor."

Bomb Baby

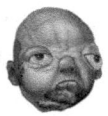

At Hiroshima University's psychiatric clinic, the old gate-keeper is puzzled at the silent car pulling up from the night darkness. He straightens his gold shoulder-braid and epaulets, and is about to come marching out to intercept the intruder. But he recognizes Professor Edwine through the windshield. The gatekeeper bows ninety degrees, and Hank noiselessly guns it over the curb.

Sam grabs the upper half of the Flame Dancer, Hank the lower, and they enter. They kick off their shoes and step into plastic slippers.

"I hate this ritual," mutters Hank.

They pass into the waiting room. Its walls are lined with pheno-barbed students, faculty and staff. The walls are unadorned gray concrete, moldy here and there. A single-sex toilet is damply squeezed in a corner, its saloon doors affording a full view of the urinal.

Hank continues grousing. "If you ever need to be reminded that you're living in Asia, just visit the doctor."

Sam's nervous student is slouched in a chair against the wall. This boy is still dressed in the same WWII-style military uniform that he wore while marching with his fellow fascists on the riverbank. Toxic Ohtagawa mud is caked halfway up his scrawny calves.

A maturely attractive night-shift nurse observes the Americans' entrance from her post. She leads them down a gloomy, low-slung corridor to a tatami room, and has them lay the flame dancer out on a futon. Sam doesn't forget to gently tuck the boy's opium pipe nearby.

Hank leers at the nurse, who looks straight into his eyes.

"It's party time, I think."

Hank drags Sam back out to the car, forgetting to put his shoes back on, and ruining his socks on the asphalt. He rummages around in the trunk.

"Seduction kit, seduction kit... where the hell—ah! Here it is." He tucks bottles of mescal and absinthe under one arm, then ferrets out a Swiss army officer's pocketknife.

"Universal lock pick. Just in case old Lotus Blossom in there doesn't have the key to the medicine cabinet... So, let's misbehave, Mr. Polly."

"Somebody should watch over the boy. You go on without me."

"Okay, go ahead and be that way. Like the syphilitic philosopher said: *What doesn't destroy me makes me horny.* Maybe you should sort of poke around for our mascot, just so you can tell Madame Edwine that you didn't waste the whole night mooning over a crispy corpse."

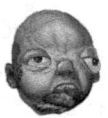

Sam crouches on the floor next to the flame dancer. He tries not to listen to Hank's voice, which is echoing up the corridor—

Bomb Baby

"Everybody knows they've been feasible for years. Why do you think you didn't hear me pull up? That baby parked outside isn't even a prototype. It's just my personal toy..."

Hank is sitting on a futon in another tatami room, fully clothed. The nurse is at his side, yawning and bored. Very nervously, he bends her ear.

"I've personally accepted bribes from a major oil company to help cap the technology. My bosses are all investing in Canada and Siberia. There's plenty of untapped oil up there ready to be sucked off like honey as soon as the tundra melts. So bring on the greenhouse effect! Speaking of atmospheric warming, how do you like these beverages, my dear?"

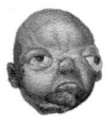

Sam tries to plump up the boy's rice-bran pillow, and serves him tiny sips from the pipe, saying, "There, there... there, there..."

Gradually, he stretches out on the mats and dozes off.

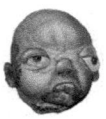

At that very moment, on an obscure stretch of Ohtagawa riverbank, the lieutenant and another thug pull the dead archaeologist from the back of their van, ready to dump him in the water.

Through the darkness comes the sound of a raft being rowed up the river.

They drop the corpse on the muddy bank, cracking its cement overshoes on a culvert. In fright, they run to cower and cringe in the van. Whimpering among blood puddles on the plush-carpeted floor, the lieutenant rubs and puffs his Shinto fetishes, and tries to bribe his countless gods for deliverance.

Sam is unable to breathe, and unable to wake up.

At dawn, Hank comes to collect him. The nurse follows. Her hair is a bit disheveled, but only a few centimeters of

Bomb Baby

the absinthe and mescal have been removed from the bottles.

Sam is calling B.B.'s name in a nightmare. Hank has to stomp on his chest a few times before he sits up, rubs his eyes, and looks around.

Nothing remains of the flame dancer but a grease spot.

"What happened to—"

"Come on, Edwine. I've got something to show you.

VIII.

Hank's car is passing back through the wealthy residential neighborhood, going in the opposite direction. Hank is at the wheel, Sam in the death seat.

"So, Edwine, guess who we decided to recruit for our sales force this year."

Sam mumbles to himself, "I shouldn't be surprised."

"I asked you a question."

"You son-of-a-bitch."

"You got that right." Hank beams at himself in the rearview mirror.

He parks just down the block from the dope peddling bum, who's still stationed behind the bush, having camped there. And, sure enough, Hank is right about bums being invisible to affluent native eyes. A teenager's father cruises right past in a silver Mercedes and sees nothing. Hank is also right about Hiroshima cops. A couple of them blunder by in a patrol car, just as blindly.

A uniformed high school girl, on the other hand, sees the bum well enough. She drops her overstuffed book satchel in the gutter, and makes a beeline for him.

Bomb Baby

"Now, let's pause a moment," says Hank, "and have a look at that employee. We've come all the way here to check up on him, so..."

Having given little bags of dope to two or three teenagers, the bum is trying to collect money from them. They ignore his pleas for payment.

"I could point out countless flaws. But, guess what? There's a certain mutual pal of ours whose sales technique shares none of those imperfections."

"You're lying. I've seen the natives scatter at B.B.'s approach. Even the tough Yakuza fear him. They think he's an evil spirit in disguise. Nobody in town could be less suited for your sales brigade than—"

"I'm afraid you're wrong about that. The younger generation have shed a good deal of their fathers' superstition. I chalk it up to the wholesome influence of American culture. Take the Keloid Krowd, for example. They didn't fear our mascot in the slightest. And neither did the coddled kids of this neighborhood. In fact, they thronged to him."

Hank begins to paint a word picture of the bomb baby's days as a dope peddler—

He's at his sales position in the bamboo grove which Mamoon and Imelda visited. His raft has been run aground, and the teenagers are descending on him. He's fetching Mamoon's designer drug from the superstructure and handing it out in exchange for ten thousand yen bills. His behavior has a definite dog-like quality. There's almost no human intelligence involved. Someone has taken the trouble to train him very patiently.

Sam says, "I couldn't even get the little idiot to hold a fishing pole. How could you and Mamoon teach him to—"

"We employed Pavlovian means."

"What the hell is that supposed to mean?"

"I'll give you a hint. We needed a woman."

"Oh, Christ."

"No, just a woman. It had to be someone willing to, shall we say, positively reinforce the bomb baby, on cue, every time he fetched bags in response to money in dry runs..."

Sam doesn't want to, but he is persuaded to imagine some terrible things that have gone on in Hiroshima—

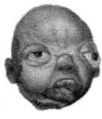

In the crypt chapel, Father Gaudi is delivering a homily from the pulpit. Polly prays in the congregation.

Bomb Baby

Hank creeps on his haunches from pew to pew, whispering into the ears of certain females.

"Figuring we could never afford a native, I personally scoured the crypt one Sunday for a foreign woman."

"Jesus. Sacrilege to boot."

"Absolute discretion was necessary, of course—"

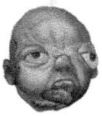

A large thug is dozing in the front pew. He almost awakens as Hank creeps over his toes.

"—because neither Mamoon nor I is suicidal enough to tackle Ishida-san on his own turf."

"You're not going to tell me you got one of the Filipinas to help you do this! They're Catholic girls, good and modest at heart, and—"

Tom Bradley

"I know, I know. To do what was required in the bomb baby's case, it took a special type of Filipina..."

Imelda kneels and weeps devoutly at the communion rail, crossing her matronly bust and fidgeting her rosary with great fervency.

Hank's car descends to the riverbank at a leisurely pace, and pulls up at the bomb baby's former sales position. It's deserted.

"So, allow me to continue my tale of heartless exploitation of the innocent... A stimulus-conditioned bomb baby was stationed on his raft behind that very mess of puckered bulrushes, there. And, not only was he able to do it, but there was something about him, salesmanship or sheer novelty, that actually attracted new kids all the time. Hire the handicapped, you know? Unfortunately, after a month or so, he disappeared with a canteen full of concentrated liquid product. Let's hope, for his sake, that he never takes a sip. His eyeballs would explode and splatter both banks... Needless to say, we'd really like to find him. And,

Bomb Baby

in the meantime, our customer base needs broadening, too. We could use your services on so many levels, Professor Edwine."

He tries to press a roll of money into Sam's hand.

"Mamoon allocated the funds himself. Five hundred thousand yen. Crisp, new banknotes."

Sam looks at the money as though it's a dead rat.

"If you're too pure and good for our money, I'm sure you're not interested in this free month's supply I was about to offer you." He stashes a packet of dope in the glove compartment. "But maybe you could see your way clear to accepting this—"

Hank hands over a waist-up polaroid of the bomb baby undergoing behavior modification. The curly top of Imelda's head is visible at the bottom of the picture, undulating itself out of focus as she performs fellatio on him. In the bomb baby's eyes are the first stirrings of self-consciousness, cynicism and greed.

"You were the one pushing me the hardest to find this man," says Sam. He looks out the car window and sees the bomb baby's final moments in a time-warped flashback—

The dope is moving swiftly. The bomb baby has a strange sneer on his face. His eyes are focused, and he seems to look with contempt at the young addicts.

Suddenly, something startles the teenagers so badly that they drop their purchases and scramble away through the bulrushes like hunted animals.

"He was lost before disappearing," says Sam.

The college cheerleaders come marching along the flood plain in full militaristic uniform, chanting and waving their horrifying banners high.

Somebody forgot to train the bomb baby to be afraid of these young men. He fetches an armload of bags to offer them.

But they aren't smiling. They thump their bass drum, scream their fascist songs, and descend.

As if on cue, the same cheerleaders march up the riverbank and come to full parade rest in the mud about fifteen yards away from Hank's front bumper. Sam's nervous student is among them.

Hank, terrified, slouches way down in the driver's seat.

"Are these the potential customers everyone's been talking about?" asks Sam.

The cheerleaders commence practicing a wild, arm-flailing chant in praise of the dead Emperor Hirohito. Trembling, Hank peeks out from under the steering wheel at the bulldog-like cheerleader.

"They seem to be patrolling the neighborhood," says Sam.

Bomb Baby

"You've got to find poor B.B.!"

"Woe to him who gives scandal to the little ones," says Sam. He climbs out of the car and elbows through the cheerleaders. To his nervous student he says, "Look in the glove compartment. Written report due first period, Monday."

He walks off, leaving Hank alone, whimpering and trying to start his electric motor, as the cheerleaders close in.

IX.

A year later, on Easter Sunday, a spectacular wedding party is gathering at Hiroshima Cathedral. The bride is Ishida-san's younger daughter. She's resplendent in a gown of Belgian lace.

The Filipinas and their babies have decorated themselves with white lilies. They are still banished to the parking lot.

Sam fitfully dozes in the Mazda among the vans. An eye pops open. He seems to have been awakened by the squeak of the baby abandonment drawer. He sits up, looks around, and thinks he sees the bomb baby wandering like a little ghost through the churchyard.

It's actually the flame dancer. Dressed in frayed clothes, his hands and face deformed by healed-over burns, he looks a lot like the bomb baby.

Ishida-san's younger daughter recoils from him and swoons into the arms of her bridesmaids.

"The animal's back!" screams the crime boss. He storms out the main gate, toward a fleet of limousines idling on the street.

Bomb Baby

The flame dancer approaches the Mazda and raps a finger on the window. Sam, too, thinks it's the bomb baby. He reaches out a hand to verify the existence of this ghost.

Shrinking back, the flame dancer says, "It looks like we both survived our night in hell, Dr. Edwine. I would congratulate you, but I can't shake your hand. My body is unlucky. The natives won't touch someone who looks as dead as I do."

Ishida-san is in the street, screaming into a limo window and gesturing in the flame dancer's direction. Oblivious to the danger, he inspects himself in Sam's side-view mirror. Then, bravely, he limps toward the steps that lead down to the crypt chapel. The congregation below starts singing a hymn, and that stops him cold. He begins to weep.

"I want to pray!"

Sam unfolds himself from the car and stands by his side, not two feet from the steps—closer than he has ever gotten.

"I'm ashamed."

"They're obligated to accept you," says Sam. "You won't be the first Magdalen they've embraced. See? Father Gaudi is down there all suited up—"

Sam thinks he sees, at the bottom of the steps, Father Gaudi waving a crude ceramic chalice around, sloshing blood everywhere. The old priest seems to leer up at him, tongue extended.

"—and he beckons you to be seated. Don't keep him waiting."

The limo door is opening.

"You're only a few steps away from sanctuary."

The flame dancer murmurs, "You never come to mass. If you come, too, everybody will be so surprised they won't notice me."

The cannibal hymn filters up the steps, Polly shrieking on top—

Then serve thyself to Christus Rex...

Eight or nine thugs are approaching in a tight formation, led by a sumo-sized gangster who is armed with a crow bar. Ishida-san runs alongside, hysterically urging them on.

Polly sings—

Or suffer our collective hex!

Sam grabs the flame dancer's arm and is beneath the ground before his knees can lock.

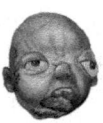

Bracing himself for the worst, Sam looks around the crypt chapel. It's the first time he's ever been down here. He seems surprised to see no blood spattered on the walls, no gnawed human ribs underfoot. Polly is approaching the lectern to read the Epistle. The front pew is occupied by thugs and Imelda.

Bomb Baby

The Flame Dancer quietly finds a bench against the back wall. He has barely arranged himself next to Sam, when he suffers a sudden fit of the shakes. He reaches into his rags, produces his opium pipe, and starts taking discreet puffs.

"What the hell are you doing?" whispers Sam. "Well, maybe it'll make you nod off. Then I can untangle our elbows and sneak off before Gaudi sprouts goat horns and breaks out the meat cleaver."

A gray haze is gathering. The foreigners are coughing, glancing back, and doing double-takes as they think they recognize their resurrected mascot. The thugs are still oblivious.

"That stinking pacifier of yours has got to go."

"But you have to stay with me. Please?"

"Listen, if you're hell-bent on making communion, you'll have to shuffle up that aisle under your own steam. Gaudi's goblet might be full of gore."

The flame dancer leans against Sam and nods off. Sam punches him, gently but firmly. "You have to be awake to take the Eucharist."

"You may not know it, big brother, but God is in your head. I'll eventually have to put him in my head, too, if I'm going up to Heaven without my body. But for now I need him inside me, here."

The flame dancer rubs his belly. He looks sadly toward the front of the church, then down at his rubbery legs. Father Gaudi reaches out his hand and beckons this small soul toward home. The flame dancer starts to nod off again.

Tom Bradley

Sam takes his elbow and proceeds slowly up the aisle, his other hand around the child's shoulder. Behind them, shrieks are heard as the thugs scramble for the exit in superstitious horror.

The familiar wedding march from Lohengrin rumbles down on everybody's heads from the church upstairs.

"Here we go, little brother," says Sam.

AFTERWORD

He is matrilaterally descended from an earlier Nagasaki expatriate, Thomas Glover, the "Scottish Samurai." Known as the Founder of Modern Japan, Glover's heavy industrial pursuits eventually attracted America's second atom bomb. It's been speculated that certain esoteric activities Tom Bradley has undertaken in Nagasaki are intended as atonement for this hereditary guilt.
— Wikipedia

What follows is that speculation. Advocate writer Cye Johan paid a surprise visit to Thomas Glover's nephew on top of a dark mountain in Nagasaki, and learned how the author has taken the bomb victims literally into his breast.

And he arose, and did eat and drink,
and went in the strength of that meat
forty days and forty nights unto Horeb
the mount of God.
— 1 Kings 19: 8

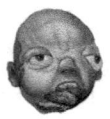

Tom Bradley

How do you go about reviewing a novel that, in the present tense, takes exactly twenty-seven minutes (a taxi's waiting with the meter running the whole time), yet, before publication, occupied the same number of reams of typing paper as the monstrosity by that other nearly seven-foot-tall Tom, which legendarily required a pickup truck to lug it to Scribner's, so Maxwell Perkins could nibble and scratch and worry its balls off?

And how do you (critical descendant of that mincing deballocker you'll never admit to being) even start to sketch out the rough draft of an essay about the so-called "Pentateuch," the new and lawless Torah, of which the abovementioned volume is but the Genesis? How even formulate intelligent questions about a splintering shelf-load of books, amounting to more than a million words—a frightening sport of nature, like all sets of quints?

You steel yourself, is what you do: you buck up your courage, fling out your bosom, throw antiquated "New Critical" theory to the wind, and seek out the law-giver himself. You try to catch the new Moses on top of his personal Horeb, before he hikes down and trips on the golden calf, after which point you'll never be able to get near him again, except for three seconds every few years at mob-scene book signings.

But how physically to locate this mountain of God? According to the promo-copy, *The Sam Edwine Pentateuch* "follows a disruptive Gargantua from the Far West to the Extreme Orient." Finding myself adrift in the latter region of our planet, I thought it might be possible to use the words of the great recluse himself as clues in a kind of scavenger hunt, Tom Bradley as the grand prize. In a recent essay published in London's magisterial nthposition Magazine (shortlisted for the European Online Journalism Award) Dr. Bradley speaks of being surrounded by—

"...itinerant TEFL trash, who are here just to stockpile money between heroin-soaked trips to the Golden Triangle."

Now there's a solid hint. It sounds as though he's been stranded, or exiled, in some East Asian hell-hole that happens to be prosperous enough, at the moment (thanks, no doubt, to America's noblesse oblige), to support a troop of those white monkeys who feign "the Teaching of the English as the Foreign Language." This couldn't be more fortuitous, because that's exactly what I am (stranded in East Asia, that is—though I guess I might qualify, in Dr. Bradley's book, as a piece of TEFL trash, too).

It occurred to me that my author and I might be within tangible reach. So I went, not bar-hopping (not just yet) but language school-hopping. I tiptoed and cringed through the dockside alleys of a certain port town on an obscure island in the East China Sea where he seems to have been marooned—at least the most recent Bradley sightings have occurred in the sordid vicinity. In dive after pedagogical dive, I kept my auditory meati reluctantly dilated for sounds fitting the following description (from the same nthposition essay):

"Almost every sentence that comes out of these kids' mouths turns up at the end, like a question, and most of their vowel sounds are schwas."

Tom Bradley

I came upon one clip-joint in particular whose closet-sized "classrooms" exuded such muffled moans. So far so good. After standing on the sidewalk outside and listening awhile, I had to agree with Dr. Bradley that—

"It's very strange to imagine them at the helms of English conversation classes. But it's reassuring to re-member that they're only working in storefront language schools where instruction is but a secondary, or even tertiary concern, if that..."

"Storefront" is right. A member of the faculty was lying on the stoop at my feet in a puddle of chemical beer, tousled braids of pork-sauce ramen swirling from the side of his mouth. Shitzu dogs serviced him like Lazarus, causing me to recall the remainder of Dr. Bradley's paragraph:

"The managers don't seem to care, or notice, if their youthful Caucasoid instructors have speech impediments, but are satisfied if they agree to brighten their hair with bleach and their eyes with turquoise contact lenses, and fornicate with the students on demand, as it's good for business..."

Hardly any dark roots were showing under the educator's regulation platinum dye job, and one of his corneal suction cups remained firmly in place (the other had slipped from between flaccid eyelids and was glistening like a sapphire zit on his chin). His adherence to the dress code notwithstanding, it was hard to imagine this comatose stud drumming up much business. This clearly was not the institution my author had described. So I decided to hit the bars and collect my thoughts. If you're going to

Bomb Baby

step on drunks, anyway, you might as well get in on the action.

I stumbled onto the right track. In a seawall tavern that offered the services of a sad gaggle of early-teenaged hand-job hostesses, some young and youngish American alcoholics said things like, "You mean that really, really, um, huge-ungus-type dude? With the sort of, like, orange beard? He never comes to drink here? But newspaper delivery guys and milk, um, men? You know? They, kind of, whisper about someone? Like on top of that, um, sort of mountain?"

A thumb was aimed over a shoulder at the largest of several dark entities that lifted their cloudy masses from among hovels in a muggy-looking suburb a few blocks inland: not quite the "backside of the desert" mentioned in that other Pentateuch, but wilderness enough for me.

Between rib-splitting coughs, a certain Englishman chimed in. (I didn't see his face because he was slouched in a dark booth and receiving a lap-job from a tiny Filipina white slave who seemed, strangely, at first glance, to have fastened her fingernails deep into his bony chest.) "If this is going to be one of those literary blowjobs, Mate, best be ready to grin and swallow when that 'orrible old cunt squirts spunk."

A subject of Elizabeth II in these special circumstances is allowed to express his thoughts in more developed periods than our own countrymen because, after all, his ancestors invented the lingo. It also helps if he happens to be the manager of the educational institution which furnishes this dive with the bulk of its clientele. I left this

Tom Bradley

Brit drilling his little lap-dancer on today's lesson, which she was obliged to recite to the accompaniment of his agonizing, chronic lung seizures:

You taught me language, an my profit on't
Is I know how to curse. The red plague rid you
For learning me your language.

I'm already tired of reporting the dialog of Tom Bradley's fellow ejectees, with whom he never deigns to associate, but who seem to have made him the main subject of their amphetamined and opiated gossip. So let me just paraphrase the remainder: stomping around on top of that geological formation in the blackest hours before each dawn, someone fitting his description (and who else in this whole hemisphere comes close?) has been glimpsed. I can't imagine how he's been glimpsed. Maybe a pair of those infra-red night-vision binocks the Syrians pilfered from our stalwarts in Iraq have made it here on the black market to please insomniac voyeurs. I doubt many people would sneak up and try verifying his puzzling presence with naked eyes. It would take a foolhardy weirdo or an obsessed stalker type, or a hybrid of both.

All that remained for me was to dig in on a bus bench and wait for the first subtle insinuations of sunrise. This did not require the *patienza* of Mother Teresa because, around here, it comes at four o'clock. The natives, who are mostly middle-class office-workers (though that's about to change, as their country relaxes deeper and deeper into the trance called penury) are not allowed to go home until the

Bomb Baby

boss does, and it's easier to make the old rooster feel guilty if it's pitch dark outside; therefore Daylight Savings Time is a taboo subject among elected officials.

There. That's all you know, and all you need to know, about the setting of this encounter. (Incidentally it's Nippon we're talking about—Nagasaki, if you insist on pinching and puckering it down even further.) Now you understand why this brush with genius has to happen on top of Horeb East, in the wee hours, elevated in space and insulated in time from the inscrutability, the misdirection, the willful uncommunicativeness, the suffocating group-pressure brought to bear with exquisite obliquity even on the slave masters themselves. So, the boss won't close up at a decent hour? Instead of rising up like other prisoners of major industrialized economies and demanding a contract with set work-hours, let's just quietly cause the sun to go down and come up again with unnatural prematurity, and meantime huddle together, sullen at our desks in the gathering gloom. Land of the Rising Sun, and how.

Why in God's name is our author here? Though craving an immediate solution to this and countless other Bradleyan perplexities, I decided for the time being to tuck them all away, to empty my head as far as possible for a non-zen master or an American over the age of twenty-five, and just start climbing blindly.

Tom Bradley

Through near-pitch blackness my way spiraled up and up, switching back and forth in the foreign air. The track's soggy surface seemed always to bank in the direction opposite to what any sane surveyor would choose, assuming his purpose was to discourage vehicles and beings from falling off the outer edge. Below, in blackish-greenness, fanged with fronds, a bamboo maw gaped and groaned with the breeze, as if some exotic category of the damned were lodged in its throat-thick stalks. And beyond that weedy perdition, steadily sinking from my point of view, our author's adopted city moaned out its own continuo to the chorus. The further each of my steps lifted me above it, the more definitely I could hear Nagasaki's song—and it wasn't Puccini's greatest hit.

Dr. Bradley's mainland neighbors have, for thou-sands of years, recognized the Root Tone of Nature. A city of any time or nation, if situated far enough away to be apprehended as a whole, produces this note, the same sung by a river in full springtime spate, or a vast deciduous forest when the wind rushes through its boughs. It is said to share the wavelength of F above middle-C on a piano well-tempered and tuned precisely to A at 440 hertz, of which there are precious few in China—and small wonder: imagine the interlocking layers of high civilization required to bring such a marvel into existence. Back in the dynastic days when this notion was formulated the Celestials were using guitar-like contraptions.

"Hast thou attuned thy heart and mind to the great mind and heart of all mankind? For as all Nature-sounds are echoed back by the sacred River's roaring voice, so the

Bomb Baby

heart of him who in the stream would enter must thrill in response to every sigh and thought of all that lives and breathes." Thus says the *Book of Golden Precepts*, as translated by the mighty Pythoness of Dnepropetrovsk—whom I've long suspected of being Tom Bradley's spiritual guide. (And if it seems strange to you that the author of such works as "Squirting Chubbies" and "Baptizing Dead People for Fun and Profit" should have one of those, imagine how it strikes me, his disciple.)

Did I hear the Root Tone of Nature on this dwindling night? Elijah was privy to nothing less than the "still small voice" when he hiked Horeb; but what about simple Cye Johan? Was he worthy of even a single sigh or thought from anything that lives and breathes? Or perhaps just a whispering hint of the "eternal note of sadness"? I can't say. But I can identify what did get my poor unenlightened timpanic membranes quivering in their merely mechanical way—and dare I admit that the Bradley-possessed "heart of me" did indeed "thrill in response" to it?

I heard "...the dogs and delivery trucks of the distant East Asiatic metropolis; the screams of prepubescent Filipina sex slaves waking chained in attics; the rhythmic sucks of police helicopters circling over some famished housebreaker; a psychotic voice bellowing into a megaphone as the rabble yawns in the face of yet another day's wage slavery; displacements, varied and numerous, of styrofoam smoke and stale fish-breath at overpopulated bus stops—everything, at a grateful distance, blends into a single sigh that strains softly like a half-dead fly against a greasy windowpane..." Thus goes *Black Class Cur*, which constitutes the reluctant Exodus of our one-man diaspora, Sam Edwine.

Gradually, on black reptile wings, this made-in-Japan counterfeit of the Big F rose up to the same small number of meters above sea level that I had already attained on foot. There it separated into its constituent frequencies, several of the higher and more piercing over-tones grinding together to form a jagged decibel wedge, the narrow end of which drove straight into the hole on the downhill side of my head. I could hear a noisy herd or gaggle or pack or gang approaching—from which of the many directions they were capable of swooping, creeping, burrowing or sidling, I couldn't say; but it threatened to surround me, the wall of cacophony upon which hell's unquiet denizens advertise their regrettable existence and trumpet their approach. And it was played not in the Daoist key of F, but something closer to deteriorated Bud Powell's key of S.

Like the foxes that have overrun the ruins of Jerusalem more than once, these hellions make many different kinds of weird noises at those times when the sun has selfishly forsaken the sky—so they stand accused, at any rate. To make that accusation plausible, their vocabulary would have to exceed any other inhuman creature's—at least those apprehensible by the usual five human senses. Some people claim the deviated beings, whatever their nature may be, took up local tenure on a certain August morning in 1945; others say they were here first, hovering in the foam even before the magma destined to coagulate into Nippon oozed up from between mismatched rocks that

Bomb Baby

grind like the molars of hateful spouses at the bottom of the East China Sea. In either case, hills like this one become particularly noisy right about now, toward dawn, much to the perturbation of superstitious native Shinto animists, as well as secular-humanist violators of the foreigner curfew, such as me.

The rationalist minority in these parts comfort themselves by positing the vociferous presence of Rikki Tikki's cousins—you know, "rather like a little cat in his fur and his tail, but quite like a weasel in his head and his habits...and his war-cry, as he scuttles through the long grass, is 'Rik-tikk-tikki-tikki-tchk!'" The assumption is that the noises must come from the throats of certain sundry razor-clawed but reassuringly material mongooses whose ancestors, ostensibly, time gone by, were introduced into Nagasaki's environs from someplace even more purulent than Kipling's Segowlee cantonment in Gujarat. Tom Bradley decrees it to have been Sumatra, probably because he likes the sound of the name—and therefore Sumatra it is.

All this can be gotten, passim, from *The Sam Edwine Pentateuch*'s Asiatic volumes. And nobody who has been transported into the upper crannies and convolutions of his own frontal lobes by the prose in which these claims are expressed will feel the faintest inclination to check the accuracy or thoroughness of Dr. Bradley's research, if any, into this land and its lore. If the natives want mongooses—more to the point, if he thinks that we, his readers, should be given mongooses—then rest assured that he will supply the most serviceable members of that tribe, and plenty of them, with his usual furious noblesse oblige. The

Tom Bradley

spatial and temporal entirety of Nippon itself puckers to less than nothingness in the presence of the consonants, vowels, syllables, words, phrases, sentences, paragraphs, chapters and books in which it has been couched, or rather entombed, by my author. We, his fans, just lie back in the volcanic quicksand and enjoy the sensation of being raped with such doctrine, and are pleased to assimilate it as gospel, secure in the knowledge that nobody with a much bigger readership (at least among our sort) will contradict our man to the particular notice of anyone whose opinion we'll ever value to the extent of bothering to make ourselves aware of it. As he is fond of saying in interviews, "I'll libel a whole race, religion, ethnicity, tribal affiliation—I'll sink a fucking continent—if it makes for a nice transition between paragraphs."

So he makes with the Rikki Tikkis. The notion of such an infestation might not sit too badly with the world-view of a bourgeois homeowner with four more or less solid, if paper, walls to cringe behind (his flesh crawling from the rodent revulsion that seems to cross the broadest racial boundaries with no loss of intensity). But it offered small comfort to a nocturnal pedestrian like me. The frisky Sumatrans, or some entity capable of doing a fair impression of them, began shrieking and dry-heaving in the nipple-deep grass on the slope below. They kept close harmony with the internal combustions of what sounded like several oriental-style motorbikes revving and rolling in concert somewhere in the distance, in definite crescendo, which I chose to ignore for the moment. Then, invisibly crossing my path, they occupied the slope above me, bringing their

Bomb Baby

stridulations with them like cicadas stirring at the close of a clammy night, or blood-sport fans doing The Wave across a stadium overgrown with vines and underbrush. I was surrounded. This prompted me to ask, out loud, the question which, in the unlikely event that the story might be true, addresses the most implausible part of all: "Who was dumb enough to come up with the bright idea to import such skittering horrors?" (I mean the mongooses, not the motorcycles.) As with all such questions, the intelligent hiker will consult the pertinent book of the new Torah, specifically *Flip-kun,* our Leviticus.

As it turns out, this being the Extreme Orient, no-body, not even sage Dr. Bradley, is able to name a specific mortal human on whom the irruption can be blamed; but credit is taken, just as the date is defined, by the living god who happened to occupy the Chrysanthemum Throne at the moment when the shipload of miniature carnivores supposedly arrived from the abovementioned booger of geography in the Indian Ocean: in this case, the emperor's sneezy-sounding moniker was Taisho. It was "his" idea. In other words, the blunder, if it was performed at all, was performed under his administration, and he wound up personally symbolizing it—very aptly, in this case, as that divine and august personage was inbred to a vicious degree, and behaved like a mongoose himself, once again according to Tom Bradley, the World's Greatest Old Japan Hand. (I'm proud to say I helped bury the former holder of that title in my Exquisite Corpse review of *The Curved Jewels.*)

Tom Bradley

Therefore, as far as you and I know and care, it is a fact, established solidly as if it were engraved three fingers deep in black diorite, that, in the Taisho era, Rikki Tikki's cousins were brought in for rat control, but wound up being much better at beating the shit out of grannies' lap-poodles instead, so were chased up into suburban hills, like this Horeb, where their kind yet thrives on the steaming contents of stray pets' jugulars. And their liberation is all the more ironic because mad Emperor Taisho himself, their rabid personification, was "kept in a cage...and let out only to get mooncalf princes on his few fecund nieces."

Furthermore, it is a Bradleyan given that the most egregious specimen of imperial mooncalf was Taisho's heir, "...blood-bloated Hirohito, of Nanking-rape fame, whose nibbly buck-teeth and rapacious character suggest that his cousin-mother must have entered upon parturition in the middle of a royal progress into the countryside and been frightened at the key moment by a gang of the helpful little verminators. By the time the nipping godlet hunched on his homunculus-sized coat of skin, the patterns for his physical build and moral makeup had already been driven from the rat- and poodle-rich downtown and were probably occupying the rice terraces with their third or fourth generation."

One can see (or, at any rate, the good doctor, and therefore we, can see) how the mythos of the mongoose was generated and encouraged on several levels by the persons and manners of the sovereigns themselves, just as the Chakravarti kings of India were consecrated by the blood of white horses, and the emperors of China were harbin-

Bomb Baby

gered by dragons and phoenixes. The bestiarial bathos is deliberate and couldn't be more apropos.

But, even though these living symbols of His Di-vine Imperial Nipponese Majesty are capable of several scalp-corrugating cries, such as the one cited above, "Rik-tikk-tikki-tikki-tchk" (at fifty paces the sound can nibble the hairs off the nape of your neck), it seemed more and more likely to me, as I labored uphill to keep my appointment with the redoubtable novelist who put all this in my head, that Nagasaki's enormous variety of nighttime snarls and cackles might be attributed a bit too readily to the feral descendants of these strangers from conveniently demon-rife subequatorial regions. If you have spent at least one night in this haggard land, you will know all too well the racket I was hearing now, and will scoff at anyone who attributes it to mere woodland creatures, rapacious though they may be.

Like an audible and perverted version of Proust's cookie, it filled my body with dismay, from the collarbones down to the callus ridges in the soles of my feet, in the instant before my brain had time to put a name to its source. On this night the local damned had chosen to coat themselves not in sleek fur, but in pocked and pitted skins which usually belong to another species of tiny monster, known, in the quaint lingo of the country, as bosozokus: "...those unemployable highway virtuosos, bringers of insomnia to an already sleep-disordered land, teen bikers who spend each night trying to play Marilyn Manson riffs on the throttles of their unmuffled rice-burners," to quote *Hustling the East*, Tom Bradley's Dai Nippon Trilogy.

Tom Bradley

Such a presence on his mountain in the wee hours was no easier to explain than the mongooses'. There was an overcrowded stomach cancer hospice lodged in a kind of duodenal kink in the foothills; and, one of their few stated functions in life being gleefully to increase the misery of the dying, this particular contingent of bozos (or however you care to abbreviate their name) had probably gotten lost on their way to or from making sure that no in-patients were able to sleep away a few moments of the im-pending day's agony. The marginally less cretinous bozos, who tend to ride somewhere near the front of the pack, would justify buzzing that sad place with eugenic theories inherited from General Tojo: one must speed the way of weaklings incapable of survival; mouths unworthy of food should be closed sooner than later (timely conceits, ripe for revival, now that this society is graying even faster than Caucasian America). The rank and file bozos, on the other hand, like all gnomes of subhuman rank, require no theory, but just do what they do for sheer dharmic spite. Possibly they derive a sort of superficial annelid stimula-tion from such pursuits, but this must remain a matter of speculation, as they are inarticulate and unable to account for themselves and their behavior.

I knew, yet again from careful perusals of my favorite author's novels, that it would be best to shield myself somehow, not so much from their noise and knives as their adulation and halitosis. In emulation of their colleagues in more sophisticated places such as Tokyo and Osaka, these troubled teens tend to halt their motorcades and gather around any non-doddering occidental in sight, chatting

Bomb Baby

him up for fashion tips, and also for practical advice on what to eat to make themselves seven feet tall, or pretty near, like a white man—"maple syrup" is what they want to hear, as trees don't lack height (an example of Asiatic thinking). Therefore, self-concealment, at the moment, became a priority, before the convoy could overtake me, whether from uphill or down.

Now, when you clamber up a hill in the suburbs of the burg which our author has famously and cruelly renamed "Boom Town II," you cannot but remain aware, at the epidermal level, of the vast pyroclastic vulcanism writhing a few inches beneath the soles of your feet. Be-sides engendering the temblors and tsunamis for which this quadrant of the North Pacific is notorious, this buried ferment sends up a tenacious mineral vapor that seems almost consciously to clutch and suck at your Achilles tendons. It retards not only forward progress but the sort of sideward mobility required when diving for cover—which, as the stuck-pig Suzuki squeals grew louder, was what I considered doing, on feet enmeshed in translucent tar. But something I recalled reading in *Black Class Cur*, the China volume of Dr. Bradley's planet-girdling Pentateuch, or maybe dreaming the night after reading it, told me that struggle was pointless under such mucous conditions, and would only make things worse, as in quicksand.

So, barely aware of doing so, and unable in any case to explain how it was done, I calmly willed the earthly bonds on my feet to loosen, just a skosh, just enough to strain credulity to a degree acceptable in a literary work of this genre (whatever that may turn out to be); and, like my hero Sam Edwine in his rollicking, psilocybin-fueled Oaxacan jungle adventure (see *ActingAlone*, our blessed Deuteronomy), I allowed the perverse gradient of the road to settle me into the downhill shadows of the soft shoulder, like a surfer shooting the curl.

There, deep in mongoose territory, I waited for the kamikaze punks to whine past from whichever direction their scale-model plastic Harley knockoffs were dragging them. Meanwhile, my hold on gravity evaporating as quickly as an adrenalin spike, I found myself sinking deeper and deeper into pulsating jungle mulch, getting moistened up to the crotch, then pits, then beard, by rivulets of cloying dew that filtered and drained like saccharine tea between acid rain-dwarfed banana trees, up-slope.

And on they came, the salamanders—not from below, which would have been odd enough, but from above, rolling in procession down the incline ahead of me. At that point I could hardly imagine what business these beings could possibly have had on Horeb's sacred summit. Huddling there in the writhing mire, I was just on the verge of persuading my mind's eye to picture my author and them in the same frame. I hadn't yet begun extrapolating a cause for their association (was he sending them on infernal errands? Under what compulsion?), when, suddenly, as if in reaction to the sheer incongruity of that attempted mental juxtaposition—and as a psychosomatic manifestation, no doubt, of the violent jealousy it caused me (I, his Boswell, had traveled this far only to be preempted by un-Englished scum)—a nearly complete disorientation slammed like a leaden lid over my head.

Bomb Baby

It hovered and buzzed in particular around my inner ear on one side—I couldn't have specified right or left even at the time: something like a whole-body, planet-upending, universe-encompassing dose of Jonathan Swift's own Meuniere's Syndrome, vertigo and tinnitus in precise proportions, exacerbated in no small degree by what I can only call visitations from the other world—I mean the one on paper that parallels and surpasses this one, and must forever be closed to juvenile delinquents of any category. Like the "snot green sea" that inundates tourists' aware-ness when they visit a certain stone tower on a sandy cove near Dublin, imagery from the Bradleyan oeuvre obtruded upon and usurped what I used fondly to call "my own thoughts."

The acne brigade hadn't yet completely passed. Peek-ing between puckered bamboo shoots at nostril level, I could see the derriere garde, the inferior bozos, if such can be imagined, who hadn't managed, or bothered, to com-plete the transformation. They appeared to be com-pounded of unformed stools and styrofoam smoke, in spite of obvious labors to camouflage their semi-solid state under hair and lips dyed the color of old earwax on a Q-tip. Their exhaust stuck out behind them in furry swirls, like cat tails, and, rather than rolling, their wheels half crept, something like weasel paws. I couldn't see the avant garde, but I could hear strange splashes way down at sea level, and squeals.

Conscious that the unwheeled noisemakers, the ones with fur, would at any minute descend on me like piran-has on a dog-paddling tapir and set to work defleshing my skeleton, I decided that I really ought to run screaming out into the middle of the road, even if it meant giving a group-heart attack to these straggler-bozos.

To that end, I fought with the mud-vacuum that encased my lower self. As soon as one foot was freed, another problem struck close to home. Indigo-bellied lizards, also eager to avoid nourishing the ravening Rikki Tikkis, crawled off specific Bradleyan pages, assumed scaly skin, scrambled up inside my trouser leg, and fixed themselves to my poor perineum by means of crusty suction-cup toes—or, at any event, I had been led to anticipate such treatment by reading certain maniacally despairing fiction which gnaws at its author's exiled condition like a rat at connective tissue, and teems with as many tiny bloodsuckers as Grunewald's Temptation of Saint Anthony (a horrifying detail of which serves as the cover of *Killing Bryce*, the abovementioned Genesis of our new Torah).

I think I ran the rest of the way. Or maybe the shudders with which my sympathetic nervous system obliged me were violent enough to bounce me to the summit like a basketball in reverse. "Nature," to mangle once again you-know-who's words, "is too evident in this town. They need an even bigger lake of asphalt."

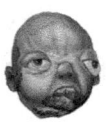

As if in an attempt to fulfill that request, the very top of his mountain has been blasted off to make room for something

Bomb Baby

unnatural. The trauma is rectilinear, but only in the vaguest way, as the edges have been blurred by volunteer vegetation. It's hard to give it a name in the moisture-thickened darkness, but the project obviously went bust, time gone by, or was aborted due to tired tribal blood. Meanwhile, giant tiger-striped spiders have grabbed the opportunity offered by rioting plant life. Hoping to profit from mongoose-horror in vulnerable ground-dwelling creatures like me, they shit high-tensile webs everywhere, thick as deep-sea fishing line, which pluck and ping like koto strings against my marauding shins, raising an alarm, announcing my approach to the author of all this crawling damnation. Enter Cye Johan, to a flourish of untuned ukuleles.

I've been hoping to sneak up on him instead of vice-versa, as that would leave me the option of changing my mind and fleeing in terror, or maybe just shambling off in embarrassment. Instead I dive into the blackness and resign myself to dying of old age while hiding behind something very odd. At first grope, it can only be described as the improvisation of a plumber with a few dozen cast-iron pipes, a monkey wrench, some time off, and an easily satisfied creative urge. No mammoth Prospero yet in evidence, I use the dead time to consider this clanking skeleton. At my touch, various layers of enamel slough off the pipes in lead-rich chips, a different shade of pastel for each receding year of the strangely familiar assemblage's existence, till the bare metal shows through, tortured and orangish-brown among the weeds. My hiding place turns out to be an antique set of tricky bars, or a jungle gym, or

Tom Bradley

whatever kiddies call these places of social resort. Little Cye just got here, and has already been put in his place.

Here's a context that clarifies and shapes the shadows beyond, and I can now situate myself, by the light of a moon that's making one final effort to look alive before the bully looms up and laughs her to nothingness. I've come to rest at the edge of the faintest recollection of a schoolyard, an abandoned country kindergarten just recognizable in ruins hanging off the opposite cliff. The tiny hillbilly matriculators meant to chatter and brachiate upon my sad tricky bars must have been carried off by malignant nature spirits during recess. Or maybe they've just grown up and begun, if not completed, the process of dying off unspawned. Even during the Pax Japonica, sukiyaki-deluxe heyday of the eighties, it's likely this whole RFD route boasted nary a pre-menopausal wife that hadn't been mail-ordered from the Philippines, and precious few of them. Here's a people long gutted. (And I'm not referring to the extra span of small intestine their senile physiologists have bizarrely hallucinated inside them, a proud peculiarity of the race, to supply the void.)

A ring of pulverized grass and atomized gravel is tromped around this flattened peak. Something enormous has been making an habitual, if not compulsive, circuit of the ragged rim. A rogue water buffalo, surely, has taken possession of this poor mountain, which can't be responding well to such rough treatment. Like the humans who failed to homestead it, Horeb East verges on dissolution even at the best of times. Loosely compounded of wild banana rot and pyroclastic sludge, softened by typhoons,

146

Bomb Baby

undermined by its own constant seismicity, this hill is prone, like all its neighbors, to the geomorphological equivalent of a nervous breakdown: the catastrophic mudslides which several times each year deform the profile of this whole quadrant of the Pacific Rim. An even briefly definitive topographical map of apocalyptic Boom Town II has never been drawn up, before or after the summer of 1945, as far as my most assiduous researches in that area have revealed.

Suspended like a mini-marshmallow on top of a poorly set jello mold, I'm scared to breathe, move, blink, or think jostling thoughts—unlike the creature which approaches now. I can hear it huff through the pre-dawn inkiness, fart and mumble, spit strangely numerous times, also snort through nostrils "the glory of which is terrible as he paws and rejoices in his strength." Inexorable as a Mack truck in low gear, it's circling around to the point nearest to where I cower behind baby-blue and pink playtime equipment. He's about to heave into my physical sight, finally, for the first time.

I can't help it. After what seems like eighteen life-times lugging around a heart and guts crammed with thousands of Bradleyan sentences, I can only find in my head two paltry phrases, and they don't even belong to him: paired prissinesses, a matched set, worthy of Scribner's nanciest scrote-nibbler, which "the present reviewer" once published in Exquisite Corpse.

I was discussing the fictional portrait of Japan's Crown Princess in his roman-a-clef, *The Curved Jewels*. I had particularly in mind the poor woman's puzzled appraisal, in

Tom Bradley

the moving eleventh chapter, of Hirohito's grandson's procreative member (which is this Divine Nation's spiritual *fons et origo*, the current incarnation thereof, and strictly speaking shouldn't be treated any more flippantly than, say, Jesus' flaccid corpus is bandied about within Christendom). The passage runs as follows:

"That part of the Prince had looked, to this virgin, like a formaldehyded specimen of the backwater vermin which her in-laws constantly fondled and talked about and identified themselves with in the world's eyes. Such bloodless things, spineless, pale and soggy, were all they knew, for marine biology was the field of endeavor the Imperial Family had fastened onto, in a halfhearted effort to justify their existence. She was dying to know if Caucasoid equipment also looked like something you wouldn't want to step on at low tide..."

With reference to the author's choosing to reside in the land which has deified that "formaldehyded specimen," and in consideration of his occasional but legendary run-ins with extreme rightists eager to defend that divinity with violence, I felt emboldened, on those famous electronic pages of Exquisite Corpse, to suggest that Dr. Bradley might suffer from a "megalomaniacal urge for public self-annihilation" and an "unwholesome Christ complex...which the present reviewer finds a bit unsettling."

"...megalomaniacal"? "...unwholesome"? Can anyone blame "the present reviewer" if he finds his own pedantry "a bit unsettling" at the moment? If you were "unsettled" as "the present reviewer," wouldn't you prefer to stay put

Bomb Baby

among the tricky bars, sheepish as a porpoise drowning in a tuna net, idiot grin fixed on your bottlenose kisser?

Now's the moment he chooses to blast out of the (for him) knee-deep mist—on hooves, from the feel of it. My intellect has been forewarned about his dimensions—behemoth Sam Edwine is obviously a self-portrait. But nothing could prepare an autonomic nervous system, nothing could steel the reptilian subcortex of a mere human brain, for Tom Bradley's elemental appearance on a dark and deserted mountaintop. This is a huge biped, and hairy. I've seen hairier, but never a huger, not in person, neither horizontally nor vertically.

He's a regular one-man Hell's Angels Motorcycle Club, Boom Town II Chapter, and he rolls right past me, oblivious as a legion of bosozokus. Even while assuring myself that I'll nail my author next time around with a tough set of proper interview questions, I know very well that it will take more than one lap before I can persuade myself not to choke. Instead of acting like a man, or even a journalist, I dig in and play the voyeur. Have I climbed this far only to let Tom Bradley get away?

Clockwise, counterclockwise, I am unable to say in which direction he forsakes me, because the leaden lid of disorientation has slammed down on my head once again and twisted everything. I've caught an extra-literary dose of dyslexia. When the clouds part briefly overhead I try to read the constellations, but Ursa Major and, it seems, Orion, too, appear as in a mirror, reversed. Two of the only unchanging items in the whole catalog of mankind's visual experience are catty-whompus. It's as unlikely a sight as even a dyslexic could expect see in several hundred million lifetimes, and inspires small confidence in my own state of mind. I do see some planets, of course, just about where you'd expect most of them to be; but Mars hangs down way too close, like a bare light bulb in a shitty Japanese one-room apartment. My giant author has to duck to get under it, and even so bumps his red head. The two of them melt together into one inflamed bilobular pumpkin.

I see this happen, and have small trouble believing it. Compared to his other accomplishments, merging his head with Mars is trivial. He is, after all, Tom Bradley, the novelist who, according to rumor, has imposed himself on this Mount of God for nearly twenty years, whom the diminutive natives have no doubt been ogling from afar like a circus freak during that endless period, yet whose own attention they've distracted to a preternaturally slight degree. (My textual analysis reveals that he knows fewer than five words of their language, and three of those are hairy-carey, okie-dokie and hunky-dory.) Meanwhile, in an award-winning feature-length screenplay, in scarcely believable numbers of stories and essays (more than seventy have appeared under his name in the past four years: see the Media Page of tombradley.org), and in the final novels of *The Sam Edwine Pentateuch*, where he exhausted the subject once and for all, Tom Bradley, the walking, stomping paradox, wrote with more perception and truth about this country than anybody in existence, now or formerly.

So, if it's no longer a fit subject for a real writer, why does he stick around this bleak archipelago, especially now

Bomb Baby

that it's plummeting into race extinction, that terminal withering of the will to press on which has always signaled a nation's utter moral exhaustion? Even mighty Greek Thebes wound up with cattle lowing and grazing on its citadel; so what pitiable weasel-squeaks can our author expect to hear from the gutters of a twice-doomed toy-town like this? Assuming he hasn't died of earlyish old age himself by that time, will Dr. Bradley yet be lingering here in another ten or fifteen years, when his honorable hosts are flat on their bellies, gazing enviously up the asshole of the Philippines and sending their own dwindling grand-daughters to Manila as sex slaves instead of vice-versa? In loitering like a crow on this carcass, is our author "indulging his intellectual masochism"? (Such was the accusation leveled at him during a wild online debate at David Horowitz's fanatical neo-con/Zionist Front Page Magazine, after they were gutsy enough to publish the eviscerating essay, "Ethnic Narcissism and Infertility in Japan" —featured, like so much of Dr. Bradley's astonishing non-fiction, in the million-hit-per-month, Webby Award-winning Arts and Letters Daily.)

I'm not the only one hanging around here who's intimidated by the double threat of such a reputation and physique. Also hesitating self-consciously, holding back with craven diffidence worthy of me, is our local yellow main sequence star. That particular wimp fidgets behind a nearby peak, pinching his dick and sending on ahead a couple of expendable junior beams, pale and wan (respectively). So far, peeking between bamboo stalks, they have only been bold enough to scout out the atmosphere several

yards over our heads. That's how intimidatingly phospho-
rescent-orange my author's patriarch-whiskers are, even in
shadow, and how glaring the flushed Celtic skin stretched
across his balding dome. (Why do I feel on shakier ground
referring to his head and mine in the same paragraph than
perpetrating a pathetic fallacy on a couple of defenseless
sunbeams?)

The good doctor and I remain twilit under a low ceiling of day. Hawks sailing almost within reach (for him) are
now pointed out in light. Each of their complex markings
looks sharp as a hieroglyph on a freshly excavated graven
image. One swoops down upon the inferior plane of existence that I, at any rate, am forced to call home, and latches
onto a bit of breakfast among things that mongooses consider beneath eating. Before he's able to resume cruising
altitude, huge obsidian ravens consolidate from the resi-
dual nighttime and harass this hawk, three against one,
recapitulating their rascally behavior in *Kara-kun*:
"...flapping and pecking alongside until the hawk drops its
football-sized rat... [the ravens] are more than aerodynam-
ically capable of retrieving the tidbit in mid-air, but prefer
to let it fall down and mature awhile in the languishing
stinkweeds."

While my attention is diverted, less by nature than the
mirror he has held up to it, Dr. Bradley completes a second
orbit without incident—of the physical sort, at any rate.
But does he peer, for a nanosecond, into the vapors that
still encase me? And does he nail an affectless but soci-
opathically intense glance right into the pit of my left eye-
ball, as though in acknowledgement of something that, if it

Bomb Baby

possessed even a single atom's worth of significance, could almost be called my presence? It's clear that he attaches no particular importance to what he sees, if I can be said to have registered on his retina at all. It feels like being appraised by a hawk's lidless orb, and dismissed as unappetizing, therefore non-existent. Have I just been neutralized by a more-than, or other-than, human consciousness? Not a question calculated to settle the nerves. It's best just to pretend the glance never happened, like so much that ostensibly takes place here on the more inscrutable side of the International Date Line. Maybe Dr. Bradley has no idea anyone waits in ambush on this defunct playground.

Flitting about on the hilltop next door, clearly incapable of registering anything like my own pudency, is a colossal Sakyamuni, exoteric adipose edition. Its jadedness has been gussied up with molded-concrete blobs of representational flesh and sluttish silk, and accessorized by the broadest affectation of a tranny-style headdress I've ever seen, with iron reinforcing rods poking through at the worst possible places. The whole cetacean abortion is spray-painted metallic yellow and sprinkled with tasteless Kandy-Kolored tangerine flakes straight out of another scintillating Tom. This god (as I suppose it must be called) touts for a stupa, an off-white dome with a well-placed cowlick, which Sakyamuni straddles primly enough. Like thousands of others throughout Hirohito Land, this stupa is stuffed with the third-hand and shopworn residue of a certain Nepalese, who, we are asked to believe, was dragged across the waterless Tarim Basin, then shunted mongoose-wise across the Tsushima Strait, yet could still muster enough sheerly incarnated testosterone to shed many thousands of bushels of reliquary-quality facial hair.

That's a whole bunch more than the greatest and butchest of American novelists ever could manage, even the extra-fuzzy one presently under consideration. But, even though he's bested in quantity, I prefer the quality of my own guru's whiskers. I haven't yet gotten a good up-close look at them through this lingering steam; but his authorial portraits, online and on paper, explode in all directions with fibers of an angel color hardly approximable by any subcontinental type, pure Aryan warrior-caste or not.

A creature hovers and tickles and flitters in the hollow of our enlightened neighbor's Chunnel-sized left nostril, flirting with a Buddha sneeze that could blow Nagasaki to hell again. It's a tiny bird, much littler than the dog-fighting scavenger-hawks and carrion-ravens that squawk and screech over our mountain, but it's easy to hear his voice clear across the gorge that separates saggy Sakyamuni from Dr. Bradley. The little frizzy-feathered birdy does his morning air-gargle, a sunshine-welcoming warble routine hundreds of times more complex and eloquent than anything I've yet heard from a moonlit mongoose. The tweets and chirps are prestissimo, a series of split-second phrases lasting without rest or repeat, for three whole minutes that could perhaps have been more profitably allocated among the day's first crop of earthworms. It's like listening to a sylph with Olympic lung capacity discourse idly on Heisenberg's uncertainty principle and laugh hysterically at the same time, by means of Rahsaan Roland Kirk's circular breathing technique. Birds of this

Bomb Baby

sort (which have an English name, I'll bet) are said by un-sentimental native ornithologists to have a Darwinistic purpose for making such beauty way up there: they are supposed to be cruising for prospective fuck-buddies, i.e., mounting a formalized mating display in the name of spe-cies propagation—which is the only other permissible be-havior for organisms in a rational universe besides procur-ing food by whatever undignified means necessary, such as skyjacking half-dead rats. If that's so, their tribe has gone out of its way to select for suppler throat muscles and sharper ears than any loved or unloved soprano saxophon-ist's I'm aware of.

But who's to say a tidy nest lined with a dozen buck-shot-sized eggs is necessarily the end towards which this particular miniature brown Sidney Bechet is working? Why does everything have to be done to impress the broads? Certain old pilgrims have worked off tribal debt, and have shed those unsightly metempsychotic pounds through regular exercise. Do we require the heavy-handed burlesque of a morbidly obese Buddha to remind us that not every spirit is encased in karmic pudge? Some have earned the choice of fending for themselves, if they happen to feel like it.

Not to overextend the avian pathetic fallacy, but what if that ecstatic warbler is choosing to come on like, say, for example, an unfeathered biped who consecrates his life to expressing himself beautifully, when, for all the red-hot action he gets in return, he can do no more than posit an audience—maybe not even hoping, but just will-fully hal-lucinating them, huddled unseen and mute in the mist around his ankles, dazzled to paralysis by his song, consumed from afar with chaste adoration for him, and only him, as opposed to some prospective new and improved junior version of him that can be parturated, possessed and duly pussy-whipped?

Without having come across this notion in any of his works, and therefore confident, as the World's Fore-most Bradley Expert, that he has never published it, I am nevertheless positive, one hundred percent doubt-free, that it constitutes one of the reasons why our author be-haves so much like the songbirds with whom he exchanges mutual greetings each morning. Furthermore, I can somehow intuit, just from pondering the expression on his face, grinning or glowering, in those authorial portraits, that he himself is unaware of this reason, except as a persistent, life-informing physical sensation of near-perpetual, intense and almost perfect delight, for which I will envy him till the day I curl up and rot and die.

I tell you that Dr. Bradley has devoted his existence to writing, number one, because it's fun (I mean the big complicated fun that none of us can ever hope to imagine, except during infinitesimally brief and rare moments in nature), and, number two, because he intends for every center of consciousness, everywhere, in all planes and conditions (not just terrestrial female Homo sapiens in breeding prime) to love him, forever, starting as soon as possible, though he's prepared to wait thousands of centuries after he's dead, or even longer if it turns out to be necessary. That's the ambition he cherishes. Talk about an ability to defer gratification.

Bomb Baby

I may not be able to answer the most basic questions about his quotidian love- and work-life (e.g., is Dr. Bradley married? Is he bisexual? Is he sexual? How does he get food? Does he eat food? Is he aware that the laundromat formerly connected to the stomach cancer hospice at the base of his hill is now open to the public and would love to serve his personal grooming and hygiene needs?); but I've been clear to the bottom of all his books and back several times, and am as sure of these two motivations as I am of my own artistic sterility and terminal uxoriousness.

Then again, I could be mistaken, couldn't I? For all I know, he might not be self-expressing at all, but rather selflessly working off some kind of tribal karmic sludge—though, like most ethnic Europeans, my own spiritual intuitions remain as yet too church-blunted even to hazard a guess as to how his solitary behavior could serve such an esoteric function. The big question, for me in any case, remains unanswered: what in the name of God is he doing here? If his soul be untrammeled as that little warbling birdy's, why doesn't he fly off this mound of semi-soft shit, and put an end to the too-long exile which rankles him so?

(Our occasionally inhuman writer is humanized by his homesickness. I find this muted but constant anguish evoked most affectingly in the Harper Collins/3am Award-winning story, "Even the Dog Won't Touch Me." Sam Edwine and his saintly wife Polly—an exclaustrated nun of the Popish confession who "divorced Christ to join him" in what The Journal of Evolutionary Psychology has called "their glorious and tender hierogamy"—are shown to be the New Adam and the New Eve. Though expelled, they "carry the garden with them," Eden being, in this case, a battered Samsonite that stays perpetually half-packed as the couple takes its solitary way through the Far East Asiatic wilderness.)

Speaking of the East, my fellow shy Bradley fan-boy over there seems to be just as befuddled by all this as I am. He still hasn't waxed any braver, the wussy. Now he's starting to twitch behind his nearby peak. He bounces on one leg while continuing to pinch his dick with increasing urgency. One spastic yellow dribble spills down to sea level, staining the dockside stoops of the storefront language schools and the teenage hand-job hostess bars—as if any amount of UV radiation could disinfect those wallows of corruption. A stronger wavelength, tried and true, is indicated.

Nagasaki Bay heaves into view, out there beyond the cliff-edge Dr. Bradley is now skirting. This deepwater inlet of the East China Sea has always been the back door to Nippon, through which undesirables have slunk in an uninterrupted string, like mucus supped from a cuspidor. Today it's TEFL trash; yesteryear it was droves of pound cake-pushing Portuguese and Papist proselytizers. We have the latter to thank for the glamorous Twenty-Six Nagasaki Martyrs, townies all, who got spiritually colonized to that grotesque degree guaranteed to earn the veneration of the diseased Romish mentality. Consecrated beings, they self-consciously allowed themselves and their children to be impaled on spears rather than place their feet briefly on a pair of shellacked laths with a diapered mani-

Bomb Baby

kin thumb-tacked on. In the blood of these slavering ma-
sochists, Tom Bradley's adopted town was christened the
"Catholic nerve center of Japan." (Guess which other Japanese town called "Boom" serves the same purpose for
protestants, just by random coincidence, of course—unless
ecumenical Ialdabaoth was in a particularly vicious mood
one summer week almost sixty years ago.)

You could trade that whole gaggle of Nagasaki martyrs
for one Tom Bradley and be much safer up here. You
could throw a regular weenie roast with all twenty-six
lightweights mincing and milling about, so particular
about where they place their dainty tootsies, traumatizing
no tremulous mud membrane. By contrast, consider my
ponderous hero. Only a miracle prevents him from bringing this whole edifice down like hairy Samson. Any other
pair of human feet would be cracking under the stress of
his trot, arches falling, toes curling backwards in ultimate
rigors. But he's my road-surfing instructor, my guru in the
skill of loosening gravity's shackles, and appears to be
functioning under no special stress. He floats along, legs,
torso and head registering no reaction to the violent action
of his feet. You could say that, from the anklebones down,
Dr. Bradley is coming on like the twenty-seventh Nagasaki
martyr, the one they never tell you about, who did the
Frug, the Watusi, the Mashed Potato and the Cool Jerk up
and down a whole trunk-load of Papist gewgaws, till they
had to shove a spear up his ass just to calm him down.

Daylight creeps up from the greasy surface of Nagasaki Bay. It sidles along the docks like a Turkish merchant
seaman with unparaphrasable B.O. and offputting man-

nerisms that you can't quite put a name to. It heads uphill to Japan's second most popular tourist destination. Raised a bit higher than the sloughs of despond I visited in the first section of this essay, overlooking the bay from a terrace covered in cherry trees, world-famous Glover Garden is one fabulously pricey piece of real estate, whose rightful inheritance my author just might not altogether inconceivably have been "butt-fucked out of," as he says, with a modicum of indelicacy, whenever the question comes up in interviews. (Who's the last guy in town you'd ever suspect of being old blood?)

It happens to be the former palatial Raj-style digs of his maternal great-great-great-great-etc. uncle, Tom Glover: none other than the "Scottish Samurai," the gun-running, ecosystem-destroying, sex-slave-disemboweling, emperor-enthroning asshole whom Giacomo Puccini honeyed over in the three-hankie opera, "Madame Butterfly." The natives call him the "Founder of Modern Japan," echoing Der Fuhrer's pronouncement in *Mein Kampf*, volume I, chapter II: "The real foundations of contemporary Japanese life are the achievements of the Aryan peoples—" except Tom Glover, like his present namesake (not to say incarnation) was rubicund carrot-topped Celt, all the way back to the Druids, without a doubt.

If Dr. Bradley is pleased to say something is so, and if the notion yields him some nice transitions between paragraphs, then by all means, so be it. Who's going to check, anyway, besides some pedantic local historian, probably ex-TEFL trash himself, who managed to wangle a neighborhood junior college gig by flattering the locals' self-

Bomb Baby

importance with half-assed "research" into their past? It is, therefore, a solid, indisputable historical fact that a cabal of grasping half-caste rival cousins ganged up and butt-fucked our favorite novelist out of a proper cherry blossom-carpeted veranda from which imperiously to sip the finest green breakfast tea and survey his domains on a bay so rich in familial history.

Unjustly dispossessed though he may be, Dr. Bradley nevertheless subjects himself each morning to the lung-lacerating exhalations of Nagasaki Bay—and I can't quite yet imagine why, as I spend my own morning doing the same. Even from clear up here, it's a smelly toilet, one part dioxin to two parts methyl mercury chloride—thanks to dear old "Unker" Tom, who "singlehandedly industrialized this once gorgeous country, turning it into the toxic wasteland it currently is," according to the scorched-earth essay, "Bloodsucker of Nagasaki,"[1] written by this dead prick's great-great-great-whatever nephew, which you'd better read if you think pride of propinquity had anything to do with these clashing relatives winding up in the same town.

On the other hand, if you're looking for the answer to my perennial question, i.e., what in God's name is our man doing here?—let's just say it's a bit early for jumping to the conclusion that mere coincidence has drawn both terrible Toms together in space, if not time. Tom the Younger might not make much of a Nagasaki Martyr, but he could be seen as a Nagasaki Penitent. That hypothesis would

---

1   See Appendix One.

clear up part of our perplexity. What might have fetched him here is—well, we could call it an intense awareness of the Scottish Samurai's military-industrial exploits, and a certain unhappy identification on Dr. Bradley's part with his voracious ancestor. As so often happens with insurmountable points of shame, this could have been inverted into a matter of pride. If so, I suspect another atom bomb will be needed to knock this Moses off his Horeb. (Pyongyang's working on that.)

Until the next flash of eye-melting light, he will remain here, steadfast, spinning on this turd-colored jello mold, toward whatever expiatory end that may serve—something sort of piously ritualistic, I suppose, like non-orgasmic self-flagellation. Not yet comprehending the exact nature of the atonement our outsized Nagasaki Penitent essays here, we might nevertheless assume, on a provisional basis, the following: that as long as Japan's dwindling economic and deoxyribonucleic momentum continues to falter on, he won't forsake his self-appointed post, not until every trace of his Unker's hard work and discipline and self-motivation and entrepreneurial industriousness and venturesomely capitalistic go-getterism has fallen to pieces; not until Dr. Bradley's religio-magical spinning has somehow sent the Kirin Chemical Beer Works, the mines, the railways, the slip-docks, Mitsubishi Heavy Industries, and Glover Garden itself, all straight to the murky bottom of the bay. And, considering the headlong speed at which Nipponese "civilization" is declining, these and other submersions will certainly happen, with or without the aid of religion or magic, well within the stin-

Bomb Baby

giest actuarial estimate of what's left of Tom Bradley's life, including years deducted for obesity and excessive height (although he should get at least two decades' worth of points for cardiovascular fitness).

And, in that halcyon time to come, "...this muggy waste, un-Glovered at last, will revert to the fishing village it was before my tribal curse descended: a place where the natives can once again develop personalities (will they be able to remember how?); where they can get out the old martyr-impaling spears and have a weenie roast, TEFL trash as the main course, and just forget about forcing themselves to pretend to encompass the impossible task of learning my beautiful language (masticating it to ugly shit in the effort); where they can have time and leisure and silence to play with their children, and chat with them in their own inchoate but, I suppose, adequate idiom; and make more children, at least to the extent their exhausted bloodlines permit; and sleep eight hours a day, and work no more than that, with a two-day weekend at least; and stop their screaming and their crass imitation American-style boosterism and huckstering—" (the latter so poignantly depicted in the essay, "The Nagasaki Literary Scene," now on offer for syndication at Featurewell.com; second electronic and all other rights available—editors act now) "—and heal the hole inside them."

Then, and only then, our man's amends will be made, hereditary debt worked off, and Tom Bradley can die, alone, spent, in peace, in the dark, draped over tricky bars, etc., etc., okay, fine, I got it. Apocalyptic this and Sacrificial Lamb that.

Tom Bradley

As a second, less obvious, not to say mawkish, alternative—since we're talking ex-cathedra any-way—we also might classify his morning constitutional among the Works of Mercy, though not strictly "corporeal" in the catechistic sense. To clarify this proposition, let's consult the man himself—I mean his words, spoken live. Let's squat awhile longer among the tricky bars and listen to what he gasps and rants as he jogs.

For posterity's sake, he happens to hold, in a hand huge, glowing and white as any pagan's chryselephantine hallucination, a Sony micro-cassette tape recorder, which he employs to play himself back every few phrases. One is reminded of Frau Forster's older brother, filling a notebook with aphorisms and constant emendations thereof, while wandering along the brisk Alpine foothills. But our philosopher has reached his summit, and is doing a liturgical dance, having changed the linear hiker's notebook for a whirling mechanism on which to spool and unspool mantras received and given. Here is a prayer wheel far trimmer and more serviceable than the Nepalese-style clunker, about the size of a carny thrill-ride, being swished about by Miss Queerbait Tangerine-Flake Buddha next door. When its reverse button is pushed, Dr. Bradley's compact appliance makes the sounds of words inhaled and taken back, difficult to distinguish from the circularly breathed chirps and tweets of Sakyamuni's feathery booger across the gorge.

I can eavesdrop most effectively on what he replays when he's tracing my particular arc of the grand cycle on his gigantic all-weather radial tire-soled sandals, retreads sloughed in arcs from still other wheels, satellites within orbits in various states of decay. Here are the first, and almost the last, words I have ever heard my interview subject say (he sounds even more like Orson Welles in the flesh than on RealPlayer):

"The dragon's mustache mirrors mine. A commissioned portrait of the one I inherited, it originally occupied the upper lip of my blood Unker, my spitting image, the Bloodsucker, who founded, along with countless other dark satanic mills on the brim of our bay, the so-called brewery that excretes the piss that fills the cans upon which the golden-mustachioed dragon struts, less avatar than advert.

"One mark of his death-dodging pride is this transplantation of his facial hair onto the flying snake's muzzle, thus claiming and bruiting abroad for himself the status of adept, or magus—he put the Naga in -saki. This is not implausible if we assume he took the left path. Look around you. His prideful works were more than human, yet less than a generation after their completion from the ground up, they were cast down, with the requisite confounding of tongues—hence the TEFL trash infestation. His stomping grounds were consumed in flames of retributive Nemesis.

"All the political damage he did, more than 10,000 normal men's worth, did not satisfy him. It wasn't enough that he riled up the pithecoid samurai; not sufficient that he put the nibbling Mongoose Family on the throne, resulting in all of Greater East Asia being flooded in blood. I'm sure he found wreaking mischief among these easy marks about as challenging as shaking insects in a Mason jar to

Tom Bradley

see if they'll fight. But I notice he didn't feel quite up to attempting such incitement among vigorous occidental tribes and nations. Then again, on a literary level, neither does his nephew, the habitual East Asian expatriate, who, likewise unable to make his mark in the real world, hides out on the wrong side of the International Date Line, instead of engaging his own civilization head-on..."

(Tom Bradley's fans, demurring at such self-effacement, disarming though it may be, will point out that the first two mighty volumes of *The Sam Edwine Pentateuch* are set squarely nowhere else than America, and have engaged some of the best heads of that civilization. No less a personage than Stanley Elkin found *Acting Alone* to have "an incredible energy level," and R.V. Cassill said, "The contemporaries of Michelangelo found it useful to employ the term 'terribilita' to characterize some of the expressions of his genius, and I will quote it here to sum up the shocking impact of this work as a whole. I read it in a state of fascination, admiration, awe, anxiety, and outrage." Stephen Goodwin opined that he'd be "be hard pressed to think of any writer who has Bradley's stamina, his range, his learning, his felicity," and the great Gordon Weaver spoke of the "flawless surface of [Tom Bradley's] stylistic facility," and his "ability to walk the edge of a tone that is simultaneously irreverent and profoundly serious." It's clear that Bradley's tower reaches at least as high as Glover's. But its staircase spirals in the opposite direction, and will bring down no heavenly wrath and destruction. Quite the reverse. As for confounding of tongues, the books themselves lay any such linguistic anxiety to rest.)

Bomb Baby

The good doctor continues:

"Like sorcerer-Pope Sixtus V recapitulating himself with pathological rapidity as the fearsome Ahkoond of Swat, sidestepping what should have been six or seven thousand years in the devachanic antechamber, my vampire Unker jumped the normal metensomatotic rails to have another crack at what he calls life, but what I call festering. He required a second gross container for his gluttonous spirit, but couldn't fasten his soul-fangs on a lineal descendant. His only son, also Tom (Madame Butterfly's unsuccessfully aborted and ill-reared bastard), strangled the family dogs and hanged his septuagenarian self just because an atom bomb was dropped on him, the pussy. A good illustration of the ill-advisability of miscegenation with the exhausted races, and—"

Its reverse button pushed by what I can only imagine to be a forearm-sized thumb, the Sony micro-cassette recorder makes a peremptory chirp—

"Don't say 'miscegenation,' you moron. And 'pussy'? Have you completely given up on ever getting back to America? Shit. Where was I? Oh yeah—

"Tom Glover craves to take further and bigger bites out of this lugubrious landscape. But a big enough bite was taken thirty-four years after his first death. That's my opinion, and I deserve to be consulted—"

Our author suddenly switches his battery-operated mechanism to the other hand, clenches it tighter against his mustache and, in a whisper never intended for my profane ears, says, "After all, it's my carcass up for grabs."

Tom Bradley

At least that's what I think he said. Before he can hear me cry, "Huh? What—?" our fallen local aristocrat swings around again on the occult circle which he has woven thrice into the volcanic mush underfoot, and passes me by a third time—and you know how any times it must happen in fairy tales and dirty jokes. He makes more revelations into the Sony's microphone—

"It was Old Man Glover's death, and he duly died it, and he's trying to cheat it through me. But he has made a fatal mistake: he chose a body half-compounded of unmitigated Bradley, Jack Mormon renegade-style, whose nature is to cooperate with nobody and nothing. If the Glovemeister was half as clever as the Nipponese make him out to be, he'd have lit upon a less congenitally perverse set of inlaws. We Bradleys told the bloody desert dictator Brigham Young to get fucked, right up in his face. Did Unker Tom think I'd hesitate to tell him the same in deference to my mom's maiden name? It's good for opening bank accounts, but that doesn't make it the password to my temple of the Holy Spirit."

(If I, Cye Johan, were the type of scribbling academic hack to insert footnotes, I might grab this opportune moment to distract you, and me, from the frankly distressing glimpse we've just gotten into our author's, shall we say, state of mind. I would provide a little solid, non-metaphysical historical background here, just to assure us of our footing, if not his. I'd take us back to the dry, ghost-free, wide-open spaces of the Far West, and point out that Dr. Bradley's agnatic line paid the full price, plus tax, for telling Brigham Young to "get fucked, right up in his face."

Bomb Baby

I'd refer you to the masterful autobiographical essay, "Suspensions of Disbelief," yet another example of our man's death-dealing nonfiction to be highlighted in Arts & Letters Daily. Its arguments organized in paragraphs crystalline and inevitable as Eighteenth-Century counterpoint, this essay, like all his others, would stand up as evidence of our author's sanity in any court of law. So much for forensic psychology.

(For more on his paternal ancestors' courageous flippancy toward the Mormon cult, see, passim, the aforementioned Genesis of our Pentateuch, *Killing Bryce*, which, according to the promo copy, "shows the disintegration of a family of Jack Mormons who get scattered across two continents like bits of rock salt sprayed from the muzzle of a shotgun." No fewer than seven well-shaped novels intertwine in this 300,000-word epic, bouncing off one another, each told from inside a different character's mind, seven centers of consciousness generating their own idioms and idiosyncratic styles, prompting rumors of seven distinct corporeal authors having passed the manuscript to and fro—or, indeed, gossip about a certain benign schizophrenia on the author's part.

(Based on personal experience, of this very morning in fact, I subscribe to the latter suspicion, with reservations regarding the qualifier. And can you blame me? I mean, this big crazy fuck thinks a dead Scotchman is crawling around inside him—and judging from his dimensions, I'd say there's room for at least six more. I should have stayed home—Osaka, in my hideous TEFL-trash case—and just done a normal book review, full of nice, easy sentences like

169

this: "For all its bulk and problematical etiology, *Killing Bryce*'s greatest virtue is its tight structure. There are few technical feats in fiction that come anywhere near. By comparison, *War and Peace* Henry James' dismissive epithet, 'primitive.'" Back to text.)

Dr. Bradley is saying, "...and not only do I defy the mustachioed dragon, but I am allowing, no, teasing, inviting and encouraging the avuncular eidolon to pursue me, till it gets exhausted and stumbles off the track that I have stomped so deliberately close to this raggedy rim, and falls off the cliff to join the swinish legions at the bottom of the bay he poisoned. I'm determined to have been neither driven nor lured here to continue Tom Glover's career of insatiable rapacity. Rather than be the beneficiary of astral nepotism, I choose to occupy his place on my own terms..."

The voice now swells to even greater than normal Orson Wellesian stentoriousness, frightening the ravens overhead—

"For I am the Human Exhaust Fan, the Great Whirling Air Exchange System of Boom Town II."

(Well, that's one way to encourage yourself to do your aerobics every day. His resting pulse rate's probably the same as his age: extremely low fifties. A tree's going to have to fall on this guy and stun him first, then Pyongyang can have a crack at him. Or maybe the "exhaust fan" is just another of the fart jokes with which he's inordinately fond of puffing up his widely anthologized "flash fiction"—a form whose extreme concision isn't normally associated with puffing or padding. But such is the ludic virtuosity of the master: he can conjure a universe in twenty-five words,

Bomb Baby

and fritter away the remaining seventy-five teasing us like a feather up a nostril. I'm sure that's what this Uncle Soul-Vampire business is about. He's just tickling me, waiting for me to sneeze and reveal my peeking presence, so he can roar, "Gotcha!" and make me shit my pants. Big laffs.)

Tom Bradley has taken possession of this aerie, a natural fortress commanding coastal access to a downtown no less mountainous than its suburbs. From up here he enjoys an air traffic controller's-eye-view of the inlets and outlets carved by immemorial lava among the maze of volcanic hills upon which Boom Town II is built. (History's stupider choice for a nuclear strike, Nagasaki makes Rome look like Topeka.) He is in a position to help unravel these tousled braids of topography on behalf of whomever or whatever might be wandering down there in a state of disorientation.

As if in commemoration of the morning when they broiled under a much brighter sun, the snaking inner-city gorges still, in certain slants of dawn's early light, seem to flow with gamma particles and molten humans in their myriads. It's said that sudden murder of particular violence and treachery can knock astral monads off the Circle of Necessity's treadmill, resulting in unquiet dead, doomed for a certain term to walk the night, and so forth. In this case, the certain term has lasted nearly sixty years. The poor Nagasaki-jin, like their brethren the Hiroshimites before them, were sucker-punched, black-jacked, cudgeled on the noggin harder than anybody since the sage Aurva gave the fire missile to King Sagara in the *Vishnu Purana*. Their hard-won coats of matter annihilated instantaneously, stripped and disorganized so suddenly, the atomic dead got lost in the labyrinth. For about three human generations, these pulverized pilgrims have been buffeted around the gutters and alleyways, not even allowed to linger on pools that stand in drains, unable to curl once, nor yet so much as halfway, around their houses to sleep, as the latter are no less vaporous than they. With the postwar proliferation of motor vehicles, they're sucked without stint into the radiators and shat out the exhaust manifolds of numberless speeding Mazdas and Toyotas, often pureed through several internal combustion systems in rapid succession, so suicidal are the tailgating tendencies of their postmodern townsmen. They've been smutched and rendered insensate by constant adulteration with unburnt diesel fuel and other airborne hydrocarbon solids.

Tape machine chirping, our author skirts the bit of rim, opposite the bay, that overlooks Ground Zero, nestled snugly between a reductive Palatine and a bathetic Esquiline. Right about now, during the hours just before, during and after dawn, the road traffic down there is sparse as it gets in this insomniac land, and a cleansing geothermal mist begins briefly to gather and rise. The air isn't quite so thickly streaked with static electric-blue bolts of frantic, hopeless nervous energy generated by a post-war citizenry exhausted as Mexicans, but not allowed to relax and snooze away their last few gasps as a race. At this time of day, Dr. Bradley's golden hours, the nuked souls come the closest they ever get to being alive, in the sense of possessing some rudimentary approximation of will, and at least a hint of self-locomotive power, like amoebas in a dilute acid

Bomb Baby

bath with only two thirds of their flagella rendered immotile. They're susceptible to being summoned, or seduced in certain depraved cases. Swirling and shrieking like tiny songbirds with their pinfeathers singed off, they're more likely to hear and respond to Dr. Bradley's voice on the micro-tape, his words played backwards, which is inhalation. The recorder, held near his face, chirps and beckons the semi-senseless beings up the hill to the neighborhood of his nostrils, like a muezzin luring the faithful to the twin portals of the sanctuary of his respiratory system and the microcosm it constitutes.

The doctor snorts astral monads. He aspirates them in their singularity, as uncompounded atoms. And at some point during the process of metabolic gas ex-change that takes place in our genius' serviceable alveoli, they can latch onto waste molecules of carbon dioxide excreted from his own mortal coil.

Each night and morning, as far as I am able to gather, he goes round and round, rescuing defunct Nips in this heterodox manner. Just as I briefly intuited a bit earlier in this essay, he does indeed seem to be "working off some kind of tribal karmic sludge"—that portion left behind by Unker Tom, who's responsible for bringing down the greatest disservice yet done to any other town but one in the post-Mahabharatic age: he founded Mitsubishi Heavy Industries, the target of America's famous Big Boy.

The doctor allows his Unker's victims a period of devachanic rest, immeasurably long from their point of view, but only lasting a half-lap on this track, as manifested on our phenomenological plane. The particulate wretches are blessed with an apparent sempiternity inside Tom Bradley to compose themselves, to gather up as much useful consciousness as possible, along with whatever matter he can spare them, with which to seed their new embodiments. I fear he's allowing his infinitesimal nurslings to erode the delicate lining of his bronchial tubes. Physicians, who tend to be rationalists even in Japan these latter days, would say our jogger guarantees himself a world-class case of emphysema by stubbornly insisting on doing his morning workout not in a civic gymnasium with a proper air-filtration system, but outdoors, where there's pollution—thanks, again, to the Glovemeister. But amends are being made, as the victims are coddled, recruited, not to say transmogrified (just yet), by way of an occult ritual to which I am not privy, prayer wheel whirled, charms mumbled.

Bizarre conditions call for freakish measures; a man of normal dimensions couldn't do this chore. Poison Tom Glover supplied his own antidote in his enormous Celtic genes, which his distantly descended nephew has inherited and supplemented with equine Anglo-Saxon Bradleyness, and religious observation of this cardiovascular regimen, exhibiting self-discipline uncharacteristic of a scion of fallen aristocracy, which would tend to support his vocation's genuineness.

He expels the hopeful, naked little beings on a jet-blast as cyclonic as his triple-sized lungs and trampoline-taut diaphragm can blow. He launches them on sturdy vehicles of carbon dioxide as far out into Nagasaki Bay as he superhumanly can, to give them a boost, over and beyond

Bomb Baby

the lethal Styx of the avuncular docks and out into the open sea, where they might come to rest and start fresh among the corals and jellyfish and polyps.

I almost rise up from my tricky bars in protest against this sudden dip into debased exoteric superstition (there is no phylic regression in proper esoteric Buddhism)—"But," says Dr. Bradley, as though he wants me to stay put for the time being, "look whose shadow I'm working in." He gestures to saggy Sakyamuni, as if his Sony micro-cassette recorder had an eye as well as an ear and a larynx, and all three were hooked up to various orifices in my head.

It's only the Nagasaki-jin incinerated during that vast epoch which transpired within the second minute after the eleventh hour of the morning of August ninth, 1945, that concern him: somewhere between thirty-nine and seventy-five thousand of them, depending on which of several estimates you buy. Dr. Edwine has chosen to err on the side of generosity, and has pledged himself to service the full load. He accepts no responsibility for casualties after the fact, collateral damage, so to speak, such as his own dog-strangling cousin Tom (a favorite Christian name in this clan). Radiation sickness, liver cancer, the suicidal despair of the vanquished, etc., allow you ample time to pack and get tickets, and if you wind up an astral vagabond, it's your own god-damned fault.

As for those immediate blast victims too solidly mired in desire when alive, therefore incapable, in death, of riding on gaseous wings across the bay with their former fellow townsmen—gentry such as Nagasaki's wartime military bureaucrats, Nanking rapists on R and R, methamphe-

Tom Bradley

tamine-maddened twelve-year-old kamikaze trainees bivouacked at the local airstrip, and General Tojo's Thought Police, who were kicking down paper doors and burning books right up to the moment of detonation; not to mention the various sundry civilian undesirables whom you'll find living and dying under a glutinous layer of demerit in all places and times: small businessmen, thugs, monastics, naughty toddlers, physicians of most specialties, people associated in any way with those sewers of lowbrow invidiousness called junior colleges, neighborhood gossips, mediocre artists, smokers, masturbators, malcontent rickshaw boys, just to name a few—these are the ones whose spirits, due to extra layers of ethical avoirdupois, are too coarse for aspiration and osmosis. They get stuck in Tom Bradley's sinus passages.

It depends on how misanthropic you are, or pre-tend to be, what percentage of the 39-75,000 holocaustees you're ready to envision lodged among his nostril hairs and upper mucous membranes. They, and not Utah cloddishness, are the reason why Dr. Bradley is constantly snorting back letting fly. Lukewarm, they are spewed out as loogs and lungers.

No sooner do these moral inferiors with their weighty load of sin splat on the ground than, in a puff of steam, they rise to possess the bodies of low, loathsome and noxious life forms, like mongooses and bosozokus. They proceed to waste an incarnation terrorizing the sub-urbanites and staid burghers with their night cries. And that explains the noises which made me so nervous on the way up here. It was these discombobulated fuckers who finally

Bomb Baby

got fitted with coats of skin to replace those melted off their skeletons by "Harry Truman's gift of Hell"—to borrow a phrase from our author's profoundly moving contribution to the otherwise cutesy-pootsy McSweeney's Journal.

But even teen bikers' obnoxiousness is not without limits. Eventually (never soon enough to suit most sentient beings in the neighborhood), they grow tired of buzzing the stomach cancer hospice in the wee hours. In deep disgust with themselves, they begin to yearn for annihilation. This is more like the bottom of an endocrine cycle than a moral insight. They end, according to procedure established by New Testament precedent, skittering down to dissolve and rid themselves in the noxious Kama Loka called scenic Nagasaki Bay, overlooked by lovely Glover Garden. No wonder the derriere garde of what I took for bozo stragglers looked imperfectly materialized. Their name is legion, like the two thousand swine in the synoptic gospels, which ran violently down a steep place and were "choked in the sea" (not drowned, but choked: the Gloverian water is so foul there's no time for a proper drowning before the throat revolts unto death with brainstem-ripping seizures and gags).

Has Tom Bradley gone insane, or is he just working on a new novel? I suppose the two alternatives are not mutually exclusive. He's the unchainable lunatic who cries at night and cuts himself with stones among the tombs. He is exorcising Boom Town II, of course, but himself as well. Someday soon a skittering snarl at the bay's greasy brink will be heard to have a definite Scotch brogue to it. It will be followed by a particularly furious gagging and choking, and an ample splash, as of a morbidly obese and splenetic quadruped, and my author will no longer be so noticeably insane.

In the meantime, Tom Bradley, who might appear upon superficial reading to be a misanthropic, sarcastic, mean old fuck, turns out to be pure and self-sacrificing. He's worked out a way to do his Bodhisattvic bit without getting too personally involved and taking on the nurture of fully embodied disciples, which, if his reputation as a teacher has any foundation in fact, would be anathema to his very DNA—and don't think for a moment this renders my current suppliant position any less untenable than it already is. (See his Salon.com articles on the vexed question of pedagogy, "Turning Japanese" and "Bathtub Revolutionary," both published in the days before that magazine's contemptible degeneration.)

But why would he break precedent and use Rikki Tikkis and teen bikers as disposal agents instead of pigs, as Our Lord did in the country of the Gadarenes? I suspect it's in fond consideration of the wild boar-meat restaurant downtown whose kitchen he's been known to shut down singlehandedly after a series of especially taxing, peckish-making jogs up here, when he needs to take on extra protein to reline the double matrix inside his ribcage. Embosomed with the portly man's womanish dugs, he's like that ambiguous entity who "...over the bent World broods with warm breast and with ah! bright wings." He's feeling broody over what's incubating in the dark, damp womb of his loving lungs.

178

Bomb Baby

(Note to my American readers: if you want to find out how you, too, can learn to manage those guilt feelings associated with the atomic devastation of the Land of Zen and sukiyaki and Pokey Mon and small-boned, sexually promiscuous young women with baby-mouse voices, now's the time to consume the good doctor's nthposition essay, "My Public Ministry Among the Heathen,"[2] also featured Arts & Letters Daily, which blogs the absolute cream of the intellectual web, Monday through Saturday.)

And he rants something frightening which I have been told never to repeat as long as I live, especially if I want to live a long time. While embarrassed to admit the warning came via dream, I'm nevertheless skeptical, or maybe self-destructive, enough to throw you a hint. It's about another invisible fluttering intelligence of a different sort altogether, the kind you'd never want anywhere near your lungs under the best of circumstances. Not formerly human at all, it's to be counted among the sprites which were here first, hovering over the sea foam before Nippon itself coagulated from a few blobs of tectonic lava—or so, at least, an uncharacteristic and unaccountable burst of in-tuition leads me to extrapolate from what I hear being magnetized onto Dr. Bradley's micro-tape.

Philo the Jew must have been right: the air is in-deed full of spirits. There seems to be a scarcely imaginable number of varieties and ranks and orders—undines, sylphs, gnomes, you name it. The unseen universe resembles nothing so much as one of those promotional scuba

---

2   See Appendix Two.

diving videos which the Hashemite Kingdom of Jordan's Tourism Ministry shoots at the Gulf of Aqaba. Dr. Bradley rants about one particular species, which are intelligent as trained sea mammals, or pretty nearly, and are eager to run errands and perform chores for any powerful human personality, as humanity is the condition that they, like no small number of the so-called angels and gods themselves, aspire to.

Our novelist appears to believe that, through the agency of one of these inhalable phocidae, he has bestowed a whopping dose of terminal lung cancer on some unhappy local slob. He excoriates, or maybe congratulates, himself for having sent an especially plump and ravenous specimen to lodge and fasten like a coal miner or bull crab in the unnamed victim's bronchia and set about the task, apparently spiritual, but by no means intellectually taxing, of chomping down normal epithelial cells and shitting out malignant ones. In most cases no such effect could be achieved by any other means than the sort of left-handed black occultism that would be karmically fatal to anyone who employed it on purpose. But Dr. Bradley assures himself (along with any unseen listeners) that his role in this slow, smelly murder resembles an air traffic controller's more than a sorcerer's. The demon has been summoned in blameless unconsciousness on our man's part. He offers his own strictly maintained ignorance of formal conjury as proof of his innocence.

To claim the ability of analyzing in detail one's own unconscious mind's machinations without the benefit of several pricey decades on a trained alienist's couch would

Bomb Baby

be paradoxical, not to say self-deceptive, in anyone but a major novelist. The latter rare category of human possesses that overdeveloped sense of self-objectivity which makes such an operation possible. Nobody else's head is so detachable from his heart. In this way the Dostoevskis, Nabokovs and Bradleys of this world enjoy a position of great privilege: they're capable of crime without culpability.

He provides neither name nor demographics for whoever's being murdered from the inside out in such a remote and unactionable manner, and I can't imagine who it would be. The only sort of person who inspires that kind of hate, at least in my experience, is a boss. But who could be the boss of this man? I pity anyone with the temerity to set himself up as such. A tumor would be the easiest way out of that predicament. I quake to consider what politicians, hypocrites, ignoramuses and Latter-Day Saints have suffered in his essays and books—and nearly die, myself, when I try to imagine all that fury focused on a single human lung. The age-old mystery of spontaneous human combustion might just have been solved.

In spite of the blasphemous, not to say homicidal and psychotic, tenor of what's erupting from this behemoth stranger's mouth, I am very nearly persuaded at this moment to climb down from my tricky bars and register my presence, come what may. I'm motivated less by the desire to preserve this problematic personality for posterity in an unpublishable interview than by certain hissings and gnawing sounds that have started up in the wild poinsettias behind me. The hellions are saying offputting things in their broad bestial vocabulary.

Tom Bradley

I still don't know if he's seen me or not. I hope not, because it would place a strong negative construction on his next action, which is to hawk up a stringy, glossy, eggnog-colored loogy and aim it right for my left eye. I duck, hear a plop in the poinsettias, followed by a sizzle and hiss, as of a small release of steam, then a rustle, then—

"Rik-tikk-tikki-tikki-tchk..."

The horror skitters up my spine: that awful sensation we sometimes feel when truffle-tusks are rooting between our buttocks for kundalini esculents. I grab my ass and, whooping like a goose, scamper out into the path of the bus. I freeze in the headlights glaring from the top of his face. The first twelve-and-a-third of the thirty-three words, total, that I, Cye Johan, interviewer, authorial profiler, literary stalker-groupie, will ever, for as long as I live, speak to my idol are as follows:

"Denis and Tran featured my review of *The Curved Jewels* in Arts and Letters D—"

He grabs me. Can you imagine how childish it makes you feel to be looking into a face big as your whole head plus your neck and torso all the way down to the belly button and back again? It's like being shot back to early elementary school days and collared by Dad, who's about to kick the damnation out of you, just on general principles.

He drags me to the cliff edge, terrifying this simple scribbler not so much with the prospect of being flung off (nor of loosening the wild banana rot underfoot and bringing down, under our combined weight—three-fourths of which is easily his—this whole side of the jello mold called

Bomb Baby

Horeb East), as by the not-so-quasi-homoerotic surrender that the touch of his hand on my elbow elicits. Honestly, I had no idea his work had affected me in such a deep way.

He gives me a look unaccompanied by words, but explicit as if he'd shouted straight into the side of my head, "How much of that did you hear?"

Instead of replying to the question, all I can think of to do with my mouth is to ask another—the very one, in fact, that the natives put to me every day of my own expatriated life, to which my reply must always be a sheepish affirmative. Under the present circumstances, it's the stupidest question of all history, whose answer, an emphatic negative, will already be known by anyone even briefly exposed to the slightest breath of this man's reputation (and that's a considerable number: of the approximately seventeen million items his name googles, without quotation marks, Tom Bradley the novelist is always the first two, and usually the third and fourth, before Tom Bradley the Mayor, Tom Bradley the baseball player, Tom Bradley the International Terminal, Tom Bradley the Civic Center, Tom Bradley the dead Negro sharecropper's son, Tom Bradley the Kiwi kiddy book writer, et al. Add any literary term or obscenity and he's got the first two or three whole pages covered).

In the face of such utter distinguishedness, I hear myself simper, through a rickshaw boy's buck teeth, gutturalizing around an Adam's apple protuberant as the prow on a mackerel boat, "A-a-a-ah, so, Bladderly-san, you speakie za Chappy-knees, yes-no?"

Tom Bradley

His reply, delivered without pause or consideration, sounds recited by rote and is addressed more to himself than any mere intruder whose full material existence he hasn't bothered to ascertain (indeed, he looks through me, like Prospero through Ariel, as though idly entertaining the possibility that I'm one of his carcinogenic sprites reporting for duty):

"I mouth a half-dozen phonemes," he says, "but couldn't tell you how they build a sentence. I've heard rumors that they tend to postpone the predicate, as our Teutonic brethren do."

Those two sentences comprise the totality of what this century's Dr. Johnson has ever said to his Boswell. The only words he has enunciated when conscious of being in my earshot are layered into a perfectly balanced brace of gemlike periods, both rounded and complete. Have they been pre-crafted and rehearsed? For the benefit of what audience? Or do major novelists think and speak extempore in these polished terms? Can I claim them as my exclusive acquisitions?

Here, in any case, is the sole exile I've met on these islands who can say more than three of his native words in a row without dropping in a Japism—including, I am humiliated to admit, me.

I've long suspected my racial, national and tribal identity of being more or less shorn; but now my eyes are opened to my true deracinated condition as never before, just by sustaining a single absentminded glance from this banished Utahn. He has not trodden New World soil for nearly a quarter of a century, and probably never will

Bomb Baby

again in this particular existence, yet remains more American than I could be if I went straight back home tomorrow and started eating dirt with both fists. I feel diminished and darkened, and made to squint. I'm a full-blooded Asiatic by comparison. Damned here for barely two years so far, I've already allowed much more of the locality to seep into my skull and infect my soul than has Tom Bradley, destined to be cremated here.

Now would be the time, not to excuse, but perhaps to attempt to explain poor little Cye Johan's presence in this miserable country. Yes, here's the opportunity to expose this scribbler and finally disburden his load of shame onto your lap: his domesticated pet barbarian condition, his status as collaborator and traitor in this particular fizzled-out culture war. Little Cye's got himself a full-time job as token Caucasoid in an Osaka junior college, complete with automatic tenure, thanks to his mastery of Yamato groveling techniques. He's been shrugging and bowing and cringing so long that his spine has sunken into itself, his body become short. At an animalistic level, he loathes himself because more than one of his native students have managed to outstrip him vertically—and they lord their superior centimeters over him with about as much mercy as you'd expect from the descendants of the folks whom China scorned as "island dwarves" for forty centuries: "...the climax of two generations of adequate nutrition under American auspices," to quote little Cye's favorite NBA-sized author, "these kids are about, finally, to achieve their full genetic potential." Cye is here to witness and meekly applaud, from below, the physiological fulfillment of the race, which comes, ironically, on the eve of its self-extinction.

While waiting for that to happen, Cye-baby has married a Jappess because, as that big, tall, fictional racist bully, Sam Edwine, would cruelly say, he can't handle fully-developed women. Maybe Cye's just a faggot who got scared away from civilization by AIDS and hightailed it to a place where, with no manly charms, skills, or even impulses, he can have his pick of any number of non-male (hence more likely to be HIV-free) fuck-buddies, unencumbered with breasts, hips, body hair, or personalities, who, bent over and viewed from behind, cannot be distinguished from pliant boys. And his catamite wife, his butt-boy spouse, comes equipped with J-kids, and a J-house financed with low-interest J-loan (throw in a lengthy barrage of pure bourgeois J-money talk here, that couldn't contrast more sickeningly with everything noble and Bradleyan above and below). Cye's got J-legal residency, which brings the promise of a comfy J-pension and, when the time comes, a J-death, with J spilling out his ears and J oozing from his pores in the form of more cringing body language. Even his final throes will be sheepish and apologetic: watch my big white outlander's nose turn strangely blue as I gasp my last.

It's easy to see why, immediately after allowing me my precious lifetime budget of exactly thirty Bradley words, our author dismisses the ludicrous likes of me from his awareness. He continues his stomp as though just the two of us have never privately shared an awakening peak, among the world's very first on this particular day in liter-

Bomb Baby

ary history. It is clear that I've ceased to enjoy even the attenuated existence I had while his attention was semi-fixed on me. Now I might as well never have been born, except to write this whatever-it's-going-to-be. I'm left with nothing but boundless vacant space, that vacuum wake which vast people leave behind them. When someone of this significance turns his back on you, Limbo gapes. In despair, I run after Sam (make that Tom) like a baby boy dogging big Daddy on legs of inferior length, trying to buck himself up and choke out further syllables of baby-talk.

Without bothering to turn around, the doctor waves that orange-shaggy arm across the cliff and down the slope, toward his Unker's toilet bay. He's too—what shall I call it, kind?—to say it outright; but I get the drift. I had no more business climbing up here than the callow youth in *Zanoni* had poking his nose into Mejnour's forbidden chamber (almost fatally—his soul was nearly eaten alive), where he saw—

"...shapes, somewhat resembling in outline those of the human form, gliding slowly and with regular revolutions through the cloud. They appeared bloodless; their bodies were transparent, and contracted or expanded like the folds of a serpent..."

Like Clarence Glyndon, I don't belong on the high places. So Tom Bradley, the serpent's nephew, ambiguously throws or magicks me back down to my proper milieu.

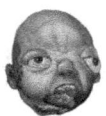

Tom Bradley

I found myself in a strange condition, mostly blind, feeling two-thirds drunk, though not necessarily with alcohol or any other compound in the repertoire of modern chemists. It wasn't easy to know where I was. Besides the green vinyl stool wedged between my hams, what clued me that I'd been deposited in some kind of tavern was this drinking song, rendered by various coarse and vulgar falsettos, squawking more or less to the tune of Mary Wells' 1964 Motown smash-hit, "My Guy":

> *I'll cling to my guy*
> *like shit to a blanket.*
> *If he proffers up his prong,*
> *I will briskly wank it...*

Though my eyes couldn't yet quite make out the vocalizers, there was something familiar about their senseless intonations, every line ending with a question mark, no vowels but schwas. Most of them were not really pledging fealty to my guy, or anyone else's, but were just mumbling and following along without comprehension, having gotten the words phonetically, because their intellects were ill-equipped to negotiate grammatical constructions at the level of sophistication favored by the major Motown lyricists of yesteryear.

It was comforting to know that I'd not been precipitated to some even more emphatically nether realm, such as the methyl mercury hell of Nagasaki Bay, but had landed in familiar territory—Home Sweet Home, in fact. Father knows best. He had expelled me back to the hand-

Bomb Baby

job hostess bar by the seawall, where I could swill and grunt with my peers, and share the meager contents of my undersized skull in simple declarative monosyllables tempered with lots of vocalized pauses. Dr. Bradley was making a statement: "These TEFL trash, and not the natives you daily fellate, are your folk."

Leading the chorus was someone familiar-sounding: none other than the storefront language school manager, our ever-coughing Englishman, who seemed still to be in the middle of the same parasitic lap dance which I've depicted him receiving in the very first section of this succinct book review of mine. His face remained concealed behind that slip of Manila flesh both darling and decrepit, belonging, at least rightfully, to the tiny prepubescent Filipina sex-slave, who had her own racial demerit to work off. It would have been better for the sad child if she'd squatted, instead, on Ground Zero fifty-eight years ago. At least now she'd have the attention of a heavy breather who could do her some spiritual good.

This manuscript was being passed from hand to semi-literate hand without my having given anyone per-mission to see the thing—which, furthermore, Coleridge- and Burroughs-wise, I had no recollection of writing in the first place.

"What kind of author profile is this?" I heard the Limey bark. "Give us his daily behavior, the details of his wage-earning life, if any. Quotidian panem, that sort of thing. You haven't shown him eating or drinking something—we like that, don't we, boys?"

"Um, yeah, you bet, boss?"

Tom Bradley

"For, like, sure, Nigel?"

"What kind of journalist is this Cye Johan?" coughed the boss (I should have known his name would be Nigel). "Too good for reality?" Then he bothered to glance at me long enough to ascertain that I was among the so-called living, and added, into my face, "You might do us the favor of mentioning, for example, certain well-known bits of common knowledge. Such as, did you know, this bloke lives in a bleeding car?" When I failed to react, Nigel decided to feign the sort of breathless, titillated confidentiality which constitutes the main contribution of his countrymen to America's current journalistic scene. He shifted to one of those stage whispers that give you tinnitus at fifty paces, and said, "Not only that, my dear, but he—"

As my eyes and head slowly cleared, I listened to him go on and on, hacking up blackish lungers the while, which the Filipina dabbed away with a wet cocktail napkin and a strange air of smug satisfaction. He enumerated the kind of snickering and no doubt true things which I did not want, and you won't be able, to hear. Maybe it's just the air of authority which a Brit accent, any Brit accent, lends to the spoken word—but my heart began with sore reluctance to acknowledge these lurid weaknesses in my ideal man of letters. I saw streaks of more than human frailty in him, such as a certain obsessive-compulsive morbidity which should have been obvious at the time, but was by no means evident to my starry eyes on the mountain, where Dr. Bradley was in his demigodly mode. Soon enough, on my green vinyl barstool, under Nigel's barrage, I began to blush, to think that suggestible Cye had

Bomb Baby

almost allowed himself to be convinced that damned souls could be recycled, if not redeemed, through someone's respiratory system.

Between bringing up hefty clumps of Southampton alveoli, Nigel said, "You silly bitch." For good measure, he added, with the kind of offhanded but utter scorn that can be registered only by people who've been living smashed together, nuts to butts, for thousands of years, "What a ridiculous idea. Snorting astral monads, indeed. Not even the sky-clad Jains imagine that."

He gave his lap-slave a kind of eyebrow-cock, as a cue that she was to laugh derisively. Though on duty, she disobeyed, and chose instead to stare at me carefully as possible through the smoke and the red particulate mist that hung around her master in place of a less unwholesome aura.

Nigel did air one bit of gossip which I chose to acknowledge here, because it has already given me one nice transition between paragraphs and promises to yield numerous more in the future. Just as I predicted in my Exquisite Corpse rave about *The Curved Jewels*, Tom Bradley evidently did, a while back, wind up getting into a fight with a bunch of Yakuza hireling-thugs. They were allegedly sicced on him by Hirohito-worshiping extreme rightists outraged over his portrayal of that dead god's grandson's penis as resembling "something you wouldn't want to step on at low tide" (as referenced above), and they got lucky enough to kill him, almost. It's not clear how many of them he sent to Kama Loka. The local "imperial" university's med school (which is supposed to be his last known place of employment; he's said to have taught conversational skills to their freshman dentistry majors—but I declare that idle bullshit) took him in, patched him up, and he woke up in the very vivisection chamber made famous on the front page of tombradley.org.

Some say that shock is what made him wind up weird as he is today—but I hesitate to ascribe such feelings of delicacy or squeamishness to my man. If he'd been born at the time, the good doctor could have witnessed firsthand the removal of our Gary Cooper-look-alike bomber pilots' living lungs, followed by the eating of their livers, sushi-style, at festive banquets under the proud Rising-Sun banner, and gotten off with half as many bad dreams as I'll take from this one-day visit to Gloverland.

Nigel happened to agree with me on this point. He ascribed Dr. Bradley's current eccentricity to another sort of trauma entirely. Winding himself up for the sort of actual sentence production that enthralled his American employees as surely as a line of spit glistening on a concrete floor hypnotizes broody hens, he declared, "Your man has been driven mad by neglect. Poor old bugger is a walking rebuke to the Yank literary establishment, is what he is. What's with your powers-that-be over there? At least our powers-that-be gave Auberon and Martin a fighting chance to rise up from obscurity. That such an artist should have to live in a place like this, among sods like us, eking out a living in one of the most degrading ways imaginable—fuck me, isn't that what drove your own Ezra Pound crazy? Seeing the best minds of his particular generation waste their vitality behind the cunting Berlitz po-

Bomb Baby

dium? No wonder he scampers about in the night air, all frantic, the sad, windy cunt. He'll catch his death of pneu—"

The last word was cut off by the expected pathological symptom. I took advantage of Nigel's incapacitation to speak up and express my sincere doubt that Dr. Bradley ever lived by teaching, contrary to the legends, the gossip, the novels, the essays, the promo copy, and everything else on and off the record. And the TEFL trash backed me up, bravely contradicting their boss (on whose lap the Filipina baby was now dozing like a puppy just come in from being injured in the gutter):

"Are you, like, kidding, Nigel?"

"The big dude a instructor? In a classroom?"

"He couldn't, you know, get work? Not with all the Japan-basher, um, stuff he has wrote?"

Nigel exploded: "He did these paltry shits a huge favor writing about them. He's the all-American high school quarterback with the golden heart, who danced a slow one at the prom with the wallflower wog who don't talkie za Amellican so goot. But is she grateful, the slag? I should think not. He's been unofficially declared an enemy of the state. I'm surprised he hasn't been deported or accidented away by some hit and run tail-gater. I've heard that his visa hasn't been renewed. He's rotted here longer than most of you wankers have sucked air, and is still on a one-year renewal. He's enduring exile within exile."

The lap dancer awakened from her junkie nod-off, and, in distressingly good English, said, "Our Sweet old Tommy's just like a restless ghost. He's got unfinished business that he can't get done, but tries over and over again, anyway. He shunts and shuffles from one Boom Town to the other and back again."

"Know what?" said her master. "Nobody cares what you think. Roll us a joint, you silly cow." At the first glimpse of cigarette papers, Nigel commenced depositing a blackish-red film of tracheal tissue on the walls and beers and people all around.

"It's Hiroshima he's published novels about, not us," murmured the Filipina in a defiant little voice as she licked a gummed edge. "But I think he was just looking for Nagasaki in Hiroshima."

The extent to which I was willing to disclose what I had learned to these profane ears was only to say, "He has a particular connection to this town."

I've seen something impossible of attainment for the usual matter-mired pilgrim, and am in danger of winding up sad as Kevin Klein's Bottom the Weaver on the morning after, but without the considerable consolation of Michelle Pfeiffer's scent and angel hairs lingering and clinging about my person in a golden fairy mist. I do have a few bristles which sloughed off onto me at the moment of contact, beastly-coarse, but seraph-hued, which I am saving in a lid baggie to show any of you, if you're ever in Osaka between now and, say, 2050, and remember to look me up. It won't be too hard to find me in the ghost town. I'll be the one burrowed in like a fox among Jerusalem's rubble.

Meanwhile, confident that the voices of this hole in the seawall will never be heard outside its confines, I, Cye Johan, who am turning out to be Dr. Bradley's full-blown

Bomb Baby

biographer, hereby, for all eternity, suppress all but one more of Nigel's whispered factoids about my subject. I've got no problems with him "living in a bleeding car," because my imagination could never place the creator of Sam Edwine between four stationary walls, anyway. So I will now, before your very eyes, cause Tom Bradley to live on wheels, just as the Limey said.

As a matter of fact, I have just decided to recollect that I did pass a ratty van on my way up the good doctor's mountain, somewhere between the mongooses and the bosozokus. I noticed it because it was covered in dents and scratches—still rarities, for the time being, even in nose-diving Nippon. Maybe he's sticking around just so he can play the trend-setter when these anal-retentives are forced by their own penury to transport their humiliated selves in rusty jalopies.

Sunken lopsidedly into its suspensions, this old van, to whose existence I am prepared to swear in the presence of a notary public, was clearly accustomed to bearing a heavy load on the drivers' side, but, perhaps sadly, none on the other. Like me, does he have an anorexically skinny wife? And scrawny kids? How can I be said to have profiled and interviewed a man when the most fundamental questions are left up in the air? Religious perusals of his works, print and electronic, yield exactly counterbalancing contradictory suspicions. I'm not even sure if the big fellow is a hetero. I could have asked Nigel, but was unable, as the word "profanation" loomed before my mind's eye like a red sign nailed to a cinder-brick wall.

Tom Bradley

I like this idea better and better the more I think about it. Living in a car is quite an accomplishment. It shows a practical-minded resourcefulness that you wouldn't expect in a literary figure, especially in this overpoliced state. Not that Japanese police do any crime solving to speak of, just peeping, aided by "neighborhood association" house-wives—which leads to the question of where he could stop and sleep. I'll work on that. Maybe I will create the greatest of all Japanese implausibilities: an unpopulated stretch of land large enough to park a motor vehicle upon without paying dearly for the privilege.

And, having accomplished that, I will wedge our novelist in his van, probably stretching him out on the diagonal. I'll let him rest from his labors, and snore as far into the broad daylight as his big dark heart desires. Then I'll skulk back to my origami house, raw-fish wife and disemboweling job.

He learned me his language. Should I curse him for it?

APPENDIX ONE

The Bloodsucker of Nagasaki

Else what shall they do
which are baptized for the dead,
if the dead rise not at all?
Why are they then baptized for the dead?
— 1 Corinthians 15:29.

There's a vampire in my background. He has stalked me all my life, but he failed to fix his fangs in my jugular until, like an idiot, I blundered into his tomb and offered up my throat. Now I'm stuck.

My mother is an opera enthusiast, but (for understandable reasons) no particular fan of libretti. She played Madame Butterfly for me on her phonograph when I was little, without much comment other than to say it was about a sad lady over in Asia. "Your imagination can make a better story," she said, "so just listen to the music. That's what I do." So, the bloodsucker missed that particular chance to invade my awareness. But then the Mormon branch of our clan scraped the clods from his face and started him up from the dead.

A couple of my grampa's cousin's eighty-year-old plural wives got bored because the old man had contracted some fresher sofa fodder, so they spent an entire summer fidgeting around in the behemoth genealogical library of the Church of Jesus Christ of Latter-Day-Saints. These sweet old ladies supplied my reluctant but polite mother with information about her bloodlines gleaned from miles and miles of microfilm..

Apart from being disgusted by the whole notion of human pedigree, my mother felt guilty about accepting the smudgy xeroxes. She didn't want to encourage this sort of thing. Like someone heating the house too much in coal mining country, she couldn't help thinking of those "volunteers" forced by threat of damnation to spend their weekends wrestling with bales of birth- and death-certificates in the vast genealogical crypt..

Such are the ant-bed-like activities in the library's nuke-proof stacks, bored deep into the granite side of a mountain near Utah's plagiarized "Zion." More than a billion dead people wait there on microfilm and hard copy, presumably with bated breath, to be scanned and burnt onto CDs and eventually baptized by proxy. The goal is to bathe in the Water of Righteousness every soul ever to visit the planet, so they'll all have a fighting chance to make it to the lower floor of Latter-Day-Saint Heaven, there to dance attendance on Mormons properly christened while alive. You can see how difficult it is, in Utah, to keep skeletons firmly buried in the family closet..

A godless cynic, such as my mother's son used to be, might suggest that this entire subterranean enterprise was actually undertaken for quite another reason which couldn't be less eschatological: to serve as a monument to

Bomb Baby

the administrative talents of a handful of men. If you are susceptible to a recent bit of flummery known as the bicameral mind theory, the Genealogical Library might remind you of the Great Pyramid of Cheops at Gizeh, or the Hanging Gardens of Babylon, any of the other preternaturally labor-intensive Seven Wonders of that historical epoch which supposedly ended, in the rest of the Occident at least, with the awakening of the side of the brain that permits individual volition, as opposed to slavish, social insect-like devotion to hubris-bloated tyrants and their egomaniacal whims. But then, who am I to sit in judgment, when my will is no longer my own, but belongs to the long-dead Ozymandias who founded modern Japan?.

In any case, my plural gr'aunties were not miffed in the slightest by anything that a hopelessly unsaved heathen like their distant nephew could say about these mighty works. They had only to point to the then-current "Roots" phenomenon and the craze for personal pedigrees among far-western nouveaux riches, to demonstrate the usefulness of compiling and preserving birth, death and copulation records from every parish church in Christendom and every pagan shrine in the rest of the world (including, unfortunately, the Land of the Rising Sun)..

My plural gr'aunties remained unembarrassed in the face of my jeering. They continued to spend most of their waking hours burrowed deep in that nightmarish hole in the rock. It's a place devoted to drudgery, devoid of decor but for a bizarre (yet hideously apropos) accumulation of Oriental shadow puppets that line the shaft down to Hell. There my personal Vlad the Impaler was waiting to be awakened. I suspect the baptismal water scalded whatever poor Mormon tried to carry his sick soul to Heaven..

Mom saw me off at the airport when, without knowing why, I moved to Nagasaki. (Somehow, it seemed to me that the sit-down job I had gotten there was an inadequate explanation for such a grotesque relocation—and I was right.) While we were waiting to be scanned for concealed ordnance, she briefly mentioned that, "according to the Mormon stuff," one of her great-great-or-whatever uncles seemed to have been a shipping magnate or something in the neighborhood of my new home, about a hundred, hundred-twenty years ago..

I had no historical context in which to place this bit of trivia. So, by all rights, the bloodsucker's name should have leaked out of my brain forty-five thousand feet in the air and fallen into the ocean somewhere over the international dateline. But it didn't. I couldn't even remember the name of my place of employment when I got into the taxi at the Nagasaki airport, but this bastard's moniker was wedged like a worm inside my gray matter, waiting to slither to the surface.

Anyone who rides elevators or avails himself of the sit-down toilets in pricey hotel lobbies in my newly adopted town cannot get away from Puccini's sad heroine. The Muzak around here always plays a synthesized disco version

Bomb Baby

of the famous tunes to which this matchless prose was set—.

They outcasting me. Aeverybody thing me mos' bes'
wicked in all Japan. Nobody speak to me no more
they all outcast me aexcep' jus' you; tha' 's why
I ought be sawry...But tha' 's ezag' why I am not!
Wha' 's use lie? It is not inside me that sawry.
Me ? I 'm mos' bes' happy female woman in Japan
mebby in that whole worl'. What you thing?

The story from which the above quaint dialog is excerpted, and upon which Puccini's libretto is based, was written more than a hundred years ago by a lawyer named John Luther Long, whose sister was an acquaintance of the son of my mother's great-great- (and maybe one more) uncle..

This uncle was a thoroughgoing son-of-a-bitch who killed everything he glanced at. A Scotch gunrunner without any of Rimbaud's redeeming characteristics, he helped restore the vicious emperors to the Japanese throne (making possible the blood-bloated reign of Hirohito). He almost singlehandedly industrialized this once gorgeous country, turning it into the toxic wasteland it currently is, by introducing the first railway locomotive and the first mechanized coal mine. And he climaxed this series of signal achievements by founding the dark satanic mill called Mitsubishi Heavy Industries, the unfortunately missed target of our second A-bomb in 1945..

Tom Bradley

Not content with raping the place, my dear old unker bought himself a sex slave from the impoverished natives, doubtlessly dickering till he got a rock-bottom price. It wasn't necessary to lie to the girl about his intentions—everybody knew the score. But he sadistically promised her holy wedlock, anyway, probably to get more sincere hip action on the old futon. He first made her a proper respectable Christian, of course, thus permanently alienating her from her family and culture. Only when she was dependent on him for everything did he leave the poor wretch (who liked to wear butterfly appliques on her kimono) with the mixed-race baby (also named Tom) whose cries were the only thing that stopped her from hacking herself to death with a samurai knife (just a short one—not one of the glamorous long ones used to impale women and skewer babies later in China, after my uncle supplied them with the steamship technology and the imperial impetus to get them over there)..

My unker left behind not only a half-caste bastard and a discarded sex slave whose belly never quite recovered from self-inflicted slashes, but also a grotesquely bloated Raj-style estate on Nagasaki Bay, with gardens that would've been big enough to provide living space for several working families. These digs were also unfortunately missed by our Big Boy in '45..

And instead of razing this blight on the landscape and turning it into, say, a hospice for the pubescent native girls who are raped and torn to shreds and infected with AIDS and hepatitis C every year by brave soldiers from America's nearby military installations, the Nagasaki Chamber of

Bomb Baby

Commerce turned the place into western Japan's number-one tourist destination. They mispronounce it "Grubber Gardens," and suppress any connection between this source of revenue and Puccini's greatest hit. They instruct the American collaborators who write their tourist pamphlets to insist that the story of Madame Butterfly is "pure fiction.".

Rather than declaring my Uncle Tom "Grubber" a national anathema and erasing him from the public awareness, chipping his name from the monuments and milestones, as the Romans did with their dead nauseating powerful people, the Japanese have posthumously dubbed him "the Scottish Samurai." They have enshrined the memory this ravenous monster, who destroyed one of their own women in return for a few orgasms, and poisoned their archipelago in the meantime. They call him the Founder of Modern Japan..

Fresh off the plane, I knew none of this, except for the melodies of the opera that, if it had a conventional happy ending, might be called Madame Glover. I was dimly aware that my mother's maiden name is identical by no mere coincidence. But that was an arbitrary bit of data floating in my short-term memory, and might have evaporated in a day or two, had I not mentioned it, in passing, during a lull in a boring but compulsory orgy of watered-down Suntory whisky guzzling in a hand-job hostess bar..

My new colleagues' eyes got wider than when you quote them greens fees in an Arizona country club. They choked up and said, "You uncle be Scottish Samurai, yes, no? You name Tom, too, jus' like you mos' bes' famous uncle, yes, no? Ah, werr-come home, Bladderly-sensei! Werr-come home!".

Now I am expected to publish paeans to my esteemed forbear, and to hold forth about him on demand at parties and faculty meetings. Having barely escaped polygamists who dunk themselves in water to save their dead grannies, I am now supposed to join my unbaptized hosts in heathenish ancestor worship. I've been urged to set up a sandalwood-reeking shrine to Thomas Glover in my apartment..

My place of employment has offered to fly in a famous calligrapher all the way from Kyoto to render my matrilineal family tree on exquisite rice paper, to be mounted under glass and hung on the wall in my office. I have only to phone my mother and somehow persuade her to dig up the Mormons' smudgy xeroxes and mail them to me..

They want me to be Grubber II, an honorary Nipponjin, like my Uncle Tom. There have been exquisitely subtle hints that I'll be given tenure in return for this disinterment of leering evil, and enough of a raise in salary to get house with a garden and a view of Nagasaki Bay..

Do you think that someone of my exhausted bloodlines has anything like the gumption to turn down lifetime employment at a sit-down gig, especially now that my children are fluent in the local dialect and can phone in pizza orders for me? The gerontocrats are planning to invite Grubber, Jr., to stay on till his prostate implodes and his teeth and hair fall all the way out, and he becomes one of them. The vampire Grub is leeched onto my neck and sucking steadily.

APPENDIX TWO

My Public Ministry Among the Heathen

...in the day of atonement shall ye make the trumpet sound throughout all your land. And ye shall hallow the fiftieth year, and proclaim liberty throughout all the land unto all the inhabitants thereof. It shall be a jubilee unto you, and ye shall return every man unto his possession, and ye shall return every man unto his family.
— Leviticus 25:9-10

I was privileged to be in 'Boom Town' (as it is affectionately known among certain cloddish members of the foreign community) on the Feast of the Transfiguration, 1995. I wore raiment of dazzling white, white as snow, whiter than any fuller's bleach could make it, in commemoration of this day on the church calendar, when Christ's three best friends watched him chat with Moses and Elijah on the mountaintop. I can't recall what trio of transcendent beings I expected to see through the brownish sulphur and hydrocarbon solids of downtown Hiroshima.

That day also coincidentally happened to be the 50-year anniversary of the event that put this town on the map while nearly wiping it off. So I took it into my head to sit in sombre reverie on one of the mass graves at the epicenter, at the very minute the bomb went off half a century before. I suppose it was a means of releasing tensions built up during the Cold War or something. And I really should not have been so surprised when it turned out that a number of other people were seeking similar relief.

Not only bicycles, cars, taxis and buses clogged the entrance to world-famous Peace Park, but tens of thousands of multi-colored pedestrians, almost all of them *gaijin* (aka 'foreign devils'). Compounding the problem were several dozen international media trucks, downright 18-wheelers, which bristled like giant sea urchins with cumbersome satellite relay gear.

To skirt this route, I decided to duck in by way of the Monument to the Korean Bomb Victims, which is segregated in an obscure vacant lot across a back alley. It was the only place within blocks that seemed to have contemplative activity going on, in spite of the well-hyped orgy next door.

Neither the tourists nor the media people were coming anywhere near this monument. Except for a few praying and singing Korean nationals, and me, their fellow unsung nukee, it was deserted. These people were pulverized by the same blast that killed all the thoroughbreds memorialized across the alley, but, having been mere prisoners of war, mere slave laborers with lower-quality fluid in their veins, they didn't deserve admission to the sanctum sanctorum.

Dan Rather was not waiting at the Korean monument to interview me. And why should he care about this particular shrine? It's only the final resting place for a few

Bomb Baby

thousand insignificant lumps of sub-humanity. An unacknowledged target of nuclear weaponry myself (and the "device" that flattened this town was an ant to the elephants that shat in my pre-teen face; I was born downwind in Utah, in the heat of the above-ground hydrogen bomb test era), I felt solidly in place at this obscure cubbyhole. I hesitated to enter Peace Park proper. Fearing that I lacked the genetic credentials, or wasn't dressed for it or something, I stood on tiptoe on the curbstone and surveyed the chaos before my eyes.

And, as usual in East Asia, I was being surveyed myself. Someone so vastly foreign is forever going to be the cynosure of every eye in this country, even loitering on the sidewalk outside a raging "love hotel" fire, with brunette adulterers, scorched and naked, leaping out windows and splatting left and right.

So, as everyone within eyeshot watches, how does this walking sideshow (let's call him Tom Bradley) celebrate the A-Bomb Golden Jubilee?

As if in preparation for a major overland trek, he shifts his weight from foot to foot, in order to get the blood flowing through his legs--which are as long as entire adults in some parts of the world. Squinting his eyes, which sting in a brief puff of combusted myrrh from the Korean altar behind him, he mutters to himself.

"I offer up my exiled condition on this poisoned and cramped archipelago. I devote my forehead full of the gory imprints of dwarf-level lintels, and my endocrine system exuding bits of decayed nuclei. With my own self, I atone for the greatest sin of my grandpappy's generation. Best foot forward. Two-three-four..."

At this moment, in Tom Bradley's perhaps slightly un-balanced mind, he can hear Max Roach blast out the open-ing drum riff from the classic recording of "Salt Pea-nuts" that was cut the same week this town was leveled. In time with the intro, this displaced Utahn shoots his cuffs and tucks in his shirt - which comes untucked again the second he exhales. Then, in time with the imaginary music, he crosses himself incorrectly, a devout expression descend-ing upon his king-sized kisser.

As Charlie Parker and Dizzy Gillespie come in, Tom lurches off, taking two steps to the bar, his foot hit-ting the petunia bed that announces the boundary of the park in precise time with the downbeat of the tune's A-section.

He moves at a brisk, skipping walk, a grin of unaf-fected joy on his face. He pauses at relatively un-populated segments of the sidewalk to dance little jigs in time with a hot riff. Nudging everybody aside with his gyrating pelvis, bellying his way through queues, literally knocking the lovers of peace and international harmony flat on their asses, this is one unassimilated barbarian.

Tom is incredibly conspicuous, even considering the greater than normal foreign presence in Peace Park this afternoon. The mood of the multitude is self-consciously morose, and it's neutralized by this single scampering Gargantua. He shouts along with the refrain of "Salt pea-nuts, salt peanuts," while gamboling along, almost float-ing. He displays amazing agility for such a mammoth crea-ture, for he is sharing in the ecstasy of the resurrected and

Bomb Baby

transfigured Christ. Tom is able to move with all the bashful-eyed, seductive grace of the tutu'ed hippo ballerinas in Disney's *Fantasia*. The effect is like the effortless skateboard-level flying one does in dreams. A shriven conscience seems to have anti-gravitational effects.

Small-to-medium-sized school children on a field trip break ranks and scatter in terror at his approach. They try to hide behind their teacher, who tells them to get back in line or the big devil will eat them up. Their larger classmates jeer, tug at imagined whiskers on their chins, stick their bellies out, and galumph along behind him.

He suddenly whirls about and roars, "Who has touched the hem of my garment? I felt the healing power go forth from my person! Which one of you little bastards yanked the tassel on my cloak? Was it you? Was it you?"

The kids squeal and retreat, but only an arm's length.

Several local office girls are standing somewhat farther along the path. They hover at a safe distance and ogle a skimpily dressed delegation of black folk dancers from Zambia or someplace like that. Yet even these preoccupied females do double takes when Tom be-bops through their midst like the Pied Piper with his youthful entourage. The office girls goggle and giggle at the American until he, or at least the lower half of him, is swallowed by the crowd; and then they get back to the feathered buttocks and thighs of the Africans.

Still farther ahead, a whole convoy of extreme rightists' sound trucks is double- and triple-parked among barbecued cuttlefish booths under the world-famous Eternal Vigil Clock, selflessly donated by Seiko Industries. Draped with vast posters praising the dead Emperor who brought hell-fire on this city, these sound trucks blare maniacal martial music and racist propaganda at an ear-destroying pitch. The aged fascists wrap their boneless gums around red and white megaphones, and scream paeans to Hitler-mustachioed Hirohito. In their radiating rising-sun headbands, they are like a hot spot on the hypocenter, a carcinogenic meltdown. The multitude weaves a wide circle around them.

Not content to be circumvented, the rightists charge from their vehicles and attack some youthful Japanese Red Army factionists, both male and female, whose identities are concealed under gas masks and crash helmets. The two small phalanxes collide in an explosion of literature, which the reds have been distributing. It is possible to catch a few glimpses of various seditious images printed on the pamphlets: mimeographed hammers and sickles, Che Guevara flashing his armpit curls, cruel caricatures of the dead emperor spasming and ejaculating ringside at the big Fukuoka sumo tournament, etc.

Both the pamphlets and the fighting are unusual for this polite city. But even staid Hiroshimites feel the urge to behave atypically on a day as strange as August sixth. It is, after all, unique but for one other in human history (that is, if you don't count a similar day the Soviets secretly visited upon the people of Eastern Turkestan in the early sixties).

At exactly the same moment that Charlie Parker comes in with his epoch-making alto sax solo, a gigantic figure blasts through the front line of fighting fanatics, cleaving this wall of humanity like a ham actor parting a stage curtain. Easily outstripping everyone by a foot or more, it's none other than you-know-who.

Tom has no political interest in anything that could possibly happen on these islands, and is devoid of civic piety in any country. He sees nothing in the rightists and the leftists but a nipple-high stymie in his path. Solely out of mild irritation at the inconvenience they pose, he uses his triple advantage in mass and momentum to bust the scuffle up. Almost offhandedly, he raises both arms and shrieks like Godzilla, scattering both sides in terror. With patronizing affection, he reaches way down and pats a couple of retreating commies on the butt.

Tom whittles a banana-sized forefinger at the funerary portrait of moldering Hirohito, whom the noodle-Nazis literally worship as a god. Over the music that blasts nowhere but inside his own brain, his mighty voice thunders cheerfully, in fluent Japanese, for the Paraclete has descended like a tongue of flame upon this gaijin's head.

"Shame! Shame on you Ojii-chan! Guilty as charged! The blood of millions oozes between your stubby fingers! Get thee to a proctology clinic! Living god, my pink and delightsome ass!" Tom grabs that body part and waddles like a goose. Four bars later, he turns and wiggles it in the deceased sovereign's face. "Cannibal god! Buck-fanged Moloch! Sink your yellowing dentures into this! Whoo-whoooo!"

Even the Red Army factionists, who feel no surplus affection for the imperial system, are taken aback at this outlander's disrespectfulness. So it is not surprising when a novice storm trooper among the rightists feels the urge to attack our narrator. Wisely, he allows himself to be restrained by his older associates, and Tom is left to prance, unmolested, deeper and deeper into the A-Bomb Day Golden Anniversary celebration.

By this point in his progress, the expression on his face has intensified into one of bona-fide religious ecstasy. Tears of joy flow from his eyes, as he periodically raises them to the heavens in beatific reverence and gratitude. On this Feast of the Transfiguration, his raiment has begun to glow like a really clean undershirt in a black light tavern. Meanwhile, the Bud Powell inside Tom's head has already torn into his unbelievable piano solo, so it's time to dance on.

He comes upon a huddle of wheelchair-confined prepubescent hemophiliac AIDS patients, hand-picked from the deep rural institutions where they will be hidden away for the rest of their brief lives. Video crews from everywhere except America are interviewing them for the wisdom that might tumble from their translucent lips regarding man's inhumanity to man. This is as close to being mainstreamed as they'll ever get in such a proud nation; so Tom drags a CNN man over, to catch them with a creepie-peepie before they're sent back to the dungeons.

To the rubber-gloved, surgical-masked wheelchair wrangler, Tom explains, again in flawless Japanese, "These kids ought to make my president really nervous. Don't worry about a thing. We'll send him a copy of the videotape, and he'll think twice before pushing the button."

Bomb Baby

Having accomplished that, Tom continues his ministry, bearing glad tidings of great comfort and joy to the benighted heathen.

He goes among a platoon of Hiroshima city cops in full dress regalia: white gloves and gaiters, silken shoulder braids, golden epaulets, and so on. With fastidiously curled fifth fingers, they roust the barefoot transients, who quietly reside every other day of the year in washing machine cartons picturesquely tucked among the azalea bushes.

A few of these bums break away and hobble over to greet Tom, their new pal, and he freely allows them to come into contact with his person. They gape in toothless wonder as they run blackened fingers over the red hairs on the backs of his orangutan hands. They stand on tiptoe, stroke his orange beard, and babble like pleased babies. Their dirt-crusty bodies begin to glow, ever so faintly, as some of our protagonist's newly acquired holiness rubs off on them.

Miraculously enough, the bums can hear "Salt Peanuts" too; so they all link arms and dance a group-jitterbug to Dizzy Gillespie's explosive trumpet solo. Tom leads them by the hand in complex figure eights and cha-cha-cha patterns on the sidewalk, constantly interposing his body between theirs and the clutching claws of the police. He yells the most exquisite Hiroshima gutter dialect down on the cops' heads, his words just audible over the raucous jazz.

"Why not let them join the party? This is their home! These cats are Ground Zero's regular and rightful denizens!" He pauses to slap a white-gloved hand away from a grimy Adam's apple. "Why are you doing this? To prettify this dump? For the benefit of today's visitors? Are you kidding? Have you even bothered to look at your international guests?"

He calls the cops' attention to the people in question. Moving in oceanic waves across Peace Park are Ivy League humanities professors, hermeneutic postmodernists, Navahos and Maoris and Ainus and such-like, along with abstract-expressionist painters and surrealist mylar photographers in their uniform beatnik goatees, plus countless wizened potters, folksingers, performance artists and moccasined English-language haiku poets, along with an entire universe of post-menopausal flower children in Nehru jackets and medallions--not to mention all the refugees from various other post-World-War-II decades, who show up in Japan on jumbo jets once a year, to invade my adopted hometown in horrific numbers, to swell a throng around the glitzy epicenter, to hold silent prayer vigils and photo opportunities and strike consternation in the hearts of world leaders who might otherwise be inclined to start a really devastating nuclear war.

Dominating an entire quadrant of this hootenanny was a twenty-foot-high memorial portrait of Yoko Ono-san's croaked squeeze. It was being adored by a multinational coven of ecofeminists, who swayed back and forth, their hands held high in peace signs. Whenever there was a lull in the rants and chants from the sound trucks, I reluctantly heard them singing, or maybe moaning, over and over and over again, "All we are say-y-y-y-ying, is give peace a cha-

Bomb Baby

a-a-a-a-a-a-a-a-ance..." They tried to harmonize in simple thirds, but couldn't manage it, and did their best to drone each other, and everybody else, into a Za-Zennish stupor.

In other words, on that summer day, exactly the wrong people were being ejected from the festivities. Our normally soporific municipal park was under occupation by die-hard Hiroshimizers, the western world's sole surviving class of people who would feel obliged to tolerate homeless types. It would have tickled them pink to be spare-changed by authentic Oriental hoboes. It was the mega-phoned Moloch-worshipers whom the police should've been giving the bum's rush to. They were the ones jeopardizing municipal tourist revenue.

By this time, the transients were filled to the brim with my communicable grace, and the oppressors had their chance to regroup and overcome their trepidation of the Caucasoid who loomed and preached in their faces. So I was magnanimous enough to permit the cops to do their job. Render unto Caesar, and all that.

As nobody at the precinct had consulted my superior reading of the crowd's mood, the cops went charging into the cardboard shantytowns in the bushes and, with their spotless ivory dress-truncheons, busted several greasy heads. They stuffed a miniaturized Toyota paddy wagon with raggedy bodies, and sped off at full siren about twelve yards down the street, where they got stuck in the same traffic jam that I had skirted via the Korean monument.

I started to wonder, as I fruitlessly scanned this Cecil B DeMille circus for familiar faces, whether I was the only reasonably sane resident of Boom Town within five blocks of this depressing shindig.

But then I saw, across the park, on top of a modest but serviceable rise, a codger in a Hirohito/ Hitler mustache, resplendent in white gloves, a silk ribbon sash, and a blood-colored carnation, which obscured almost the entire front of his boy-sized morning coat. Here was my trans-figured Christ. But where had Moses and Elijah shambled off to?

He was somberly releasing clouds of diseased doves from chrome-plated cages. Directly upon release, the poor animals, which had plastic olive branches stapled symbol-ically to their upper beaks and ankles, bellied straight into the gravel like overloaded sailplanes, to be trampled to grease spots by stampeding Hiroshimizers.

The pigeon fancier was none other than our be-loved mayor, old What's-his-name, a Liberal Democratic Party boy all the way. He was the other reasonably sane resident in attendance today, besides me, and he'd come with bells on: all dressed up in a clown suit, a deluxe boutonniere stuffed in his buttonhole. You'd never catch his Catholic counterpart down south doing that routine.

The mayor of Nagasaki is a co-religionist of my Papist wife, and a heroic man. Those rightists I saw in the sound trucks, armed with ordnance provided by the Yakuza, pe-riodically try to assassinate the mayor of Nagasaki. They've put at least one bullet in him already, because he says incorrect things about the Holy Family in Tokyo. And yet he stands firm as an eighteen-year-old's hard-on. That's how much heroicity of virtue this old mackerel-snapper

Bomb Baby

possesses. The mayor of Nagasaki is definite beatification material, a man of genuine spirituality.

And it makes sense that I did not wind up pissing away my middle years in his scenic city. As a Nagasaki "expat," I could never boast, or lament, of coming full circle in my life, of winding up in a mirror image of my Utah hometown, suffering a poignant recapitulation of my boyhood, in yet another irradiated city overrun by religious naifs and nuts. In Boom Town II, I would have no cause to compose such jeremiads in the first place. I would be obliged to serve as mouthpiece for the philosopher king--which is no way to write nonfiction with the hard biting edge that today's tough marketplace demands of a memoirist such as myself.

Philosopher king though he may be, the mayor of Nagasaki's chamber of commerce is a complete failure. Nagasaki's Ground Zero is even tackier than Hiroshima's, with its array of eyesore statuary from various other vanquished burgs across the globe. You wouldn't catch Michael Jackson laying wreaths at their hypocenter. Or even Mother Teresa, for that matter (if she wasn't already sitting on the right hand of our Heavenly Father) - although I guess it depends on how much money you slipped her, and whether you could score enough amyl nitrate poppers to keep her happy on the plane, and whether you could recruit a couple really cute Filipina pinkies who were willing to dress up like nunnery novices and let her whip their naked bottoms with a rosary and gnaw on their toes in the hotel.

Tom Bradley

Yes, I have spent years with my head buried deep in the umbilicus of postmodernism, glamorous Boom Town. Once a year in the summer, in pathetically named Peace Park, I listen to liberalism's last gasp. My fellow North American exiles assure me that I fail to grasp the sheer significance of the oddly warmish soil upon which we waste what's left of our lives.

This is it, they tell me. This is where the contemporary age began. This is where we all became existentialists, consciously or un-, where all of us - not just the philosophy grad students and the black bop musicians in the Big Apple, but each and every single mother's son of us - were finally taught to grasp Universal Absurdity.

I'll buy a big load of that.

tombradley.org

Other titles from Enigmatic Ink:
AERNI, Justin – Dead Business Men
ARMSTRONG, Forrest – Asphalt Flowerhead
BRADLEY, Tom – Vital Fluid
DANIELS, Jase – The Grubby End
FAUCHER, Kane X. - The Vicious Circulation of
Dr Catastrope
FOX, Hugh – Icehouse & Thirteen Keys to Talmud
GERDES, Eckhard – The Unwelcome Guest plus
Nin & Nan
HEAVISIDES, Martin - Undermind
JUPITTER-LARSEN, GX – Sometimes Never
JUPITTER-LARSEN, GX – Adventures on the High Seas
KONA, Prakash – Nunc Stans
LOCKE, Duane – Yang Chu's Poems
MUNTZ, Kyle – Voices
STEINFELD, J.J. – Word Burials
ULEA, V. – Snail